THE
BIG
BOOK
OF
SEARCH
&FIND®

Tony Tallarico

Kidsbooks®
PUBLISHING

FIND FREDDIE

WHERE ARE THEY?

Find Freddie along with hundreds of other zany things in these hilarious scenes.

- Uncle Sam at the ballpark
- Cowboys on the beach
- Humpty Dumpty in Monsterville
- Flying fish in space
- Peanuts at the museum
- Rabbits at school
- Flying saucers in the Old West

. . . and lots more!

Find Freddie in
Space
and...

- ☐ Angel
- ☐ Balloon
- ☐ Basketball
- ☐ Bathtub
- ☐ Cannon
- ☐ Dogcatcher
- ☐ Doghouse
- ☐ Dragon
- ☐ Envelope
- ☐ Flying school bus
- ☐ Garbage truck
- ☐ Gorilla
- ☐ Hammer
- ☐ Mary Poppins
- ☐ Meatball
- ☐ "Meteor shower"
- ☐ NASA parachute
- ☐ Necktie
- ☐ Pencil
- ☐ Pink elephant
- ☐ Pinocchio
- ☐ "Planet of the Foot" (2)
- ☐ Polka-dot shorts
- ☐ Pyramid
- ☐ Red spray paint
- ☐ Rocking chair
- ☐ Scissors
- ☐ Slingshot
- ☐ Top hat
- ☐ Traffic light
- ☐ Trash can

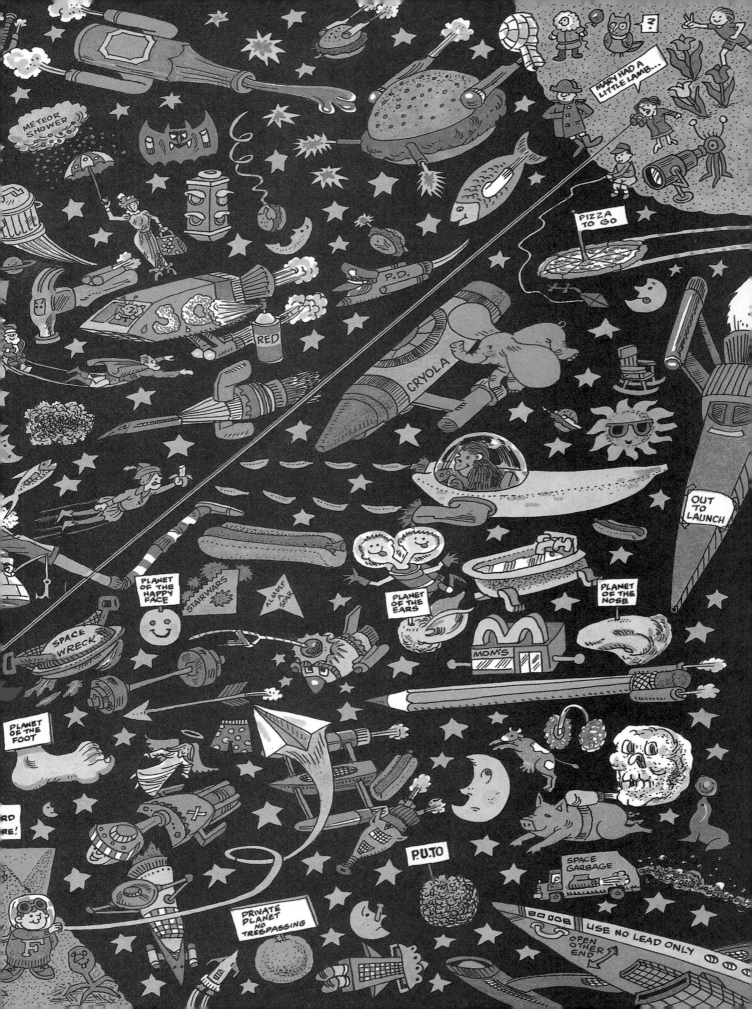

Find Freddie at the **Beach** and...

- ☐ Barrel
- ☐ Clothespin
- ☐ Duck
- ☐ Eight ball
- ☐ Elephant
- ☐ Fishing cat
- ☐ Flamingo
- ☐ Flying car
- ☐ "Fresh Sand"
- ☐ Giant sandwich
- ☐ Golfers (2)
- ☐ Handstand surfer
- ☐ Helicopter
- ☐ Horse
- ☐ Kangaroo
- ☐ Lighthouse
- ☐ Lion
- ☐ Mice (2)
- ☐ Motorcycle
- ☐ Open umbrellas (6)
- ☐ Radios (2)
- ☐ Rocket
- ☐ Rowboat
- ☐ Scuba diver
- ☐ Sheriff
- ☐ Shovel
- ☐ Snowshoes (2)
- ☐ Starfish (2)
- ☐ Strongman
- ☐ Tent
- ☐ Watering can
- ☐ Witch

Find Freddie on the
School
Bus Trip
and...

- [ ] Barn
- [ ] Baseball bat
- [ ] Basketball court
- [ ] "Clean Me"
- [ ] Dogs (2)
- [ ] Elephant
- [ ] Flying bat
- [ ] Football
- [ ] Frankenstein's monster
- [ ] Giraffe
- [ ] Horse
- [ ] Hot dog mobile
- [ ] Jack-o'-lantern
- [ ] Moose head
- [ ] Pig
- [ ] Pizza truck
- [ ] Rowboat
- [ ] Santa Claus
- [ ] Scarecrow
- [ ] Snake
- [ ] Swimming pool
- [ ] Tennis court
- [ ] Tent
- [ ] Tic-tac-toe
- [ ] Tombstone
- [ ] Traffic cop
- [ ] Turtle
- [ ] Umbrellas (2)
- [ ] U-shaped building
- [ ] Well

Find **Freddie** in **Monsterville** and...

- ☐ "13" (3)
- ☐ Broken heart
- ☐ Carrot
- ☐ Cowboy hat
- ☐ Flowers (2)
- ☐ "For Rent"
- ☐ Gorilla
- ☐ Hose
- ☐ Key
- ☐ Mousehole
- ☐ Ms. Transylvania
- ☐ Mummy
- ☐ Octopus
- ☐ One-eyed monster
- ☐ Owl
- ☐ Parachute
- ☐ Pig
- ☐ Pile of bones
- ☐ Pink hand
- ☐ Pyramid
- ☐ Rat
- ☐ Scary trees (2)
- ☐ Skeleton
- ☐ Skulls (8)
- ☐ Stethoscope
- ☐ Three-legged ghost
- ☐ Tin can
- ☐ Tin man
- ☐ Trick-or-Treat bags (4)
- ☐ Weather vane

Find Freddie
at the
Airport
and...

- ☐ Binoculars
- ☐ Birdcage
- ☐ Chair
- ☐ Clothespins (6)
- ☐ Football
- ☐ Golf club
- ☐ Green checkered pants
- ☐ Guardhouse
- ☐ Hammock
- ☐ Harpoon
- ☐ Hearts (2)
- ☐ Helicopters (2)
- ☐ Hot-air balloon
- ☐ Hot dogs (2)
- ☐ Ice-cream cones (2)
- ☐ Kite
- ☐ Laundry line
- ☐ Locomotive
- ☐ Lost wallet
- ☐ Manhole
- ☐ Paint rollers (2)
- ☐ Parachute
- ☐ Pear
- ☐ "Pequod"
- ☐ Pizza
- ☐ Roller-coaster
- ☐ Skier
- ☐ Stretch limo
- ☐ Submarine
- ☐ Toaster
- ☐ Wooden leg

Find **Freddie** at the **Museum** and...

- ☐ Airplane
- ☐ Alien
- ☐ Balloons (7)
- ☐ Bather
- ☐ Birdcage
- ☐ Birthday cake
- ☐ Doctor
- ☐ Doghouse
- ☐ Firefighter
- ☐ Fire hydrant
- ☐ "First Prize"
- ☐ Fishing pole
- ☐ Flying carpet
- ☐ Football player
- ☐ Guitar
- ☐ Headless man
- ☐ Hot-air balloon
- ☐ Ice-cream cone
- ☐ Jack-in-the-box
- ☐ Kite
- ☐ Knights (2)
- ☐ Long beard
- ☐ Magnifying glass
- ☐ Princess
- ☐ Quicksand
- ☐ Robin Hood
- ☐ Scuba diver
- ☐ Superman
- ☐ TV antenna
- ☐ Viking ship
- ☐ Watering can
- ☐ Whistle

Find Freddie in the
Old West
Town
and...

- ☐ Angel
- ☐ Apple
- ☐ Artist
- ☐ Baby turtle
- ☐ Camel
- ☐ Car
- ☐ Fire hydrant
- ☐ Fishing pole
- ☐ Flowerpot
- ☐ Football
- ☐ Guitar
- ☐ "ICU2"
- ☐ Monster hand
- ☐ Mouseholes (2)
- ☐ Outhouse
- ☐ Pencil
- ☐ Periscope
- ☐ Piano
- ☐ Pink elephant
- ☐ Rabbits (3)
- ☐ Sailboat
- ☐ Saw
- ☐ Smoke signal
- ☐ Soccer ball
- ☐ Stop sign
- ☐ Sun
- ☐ Toasters (5)
- ☐ UFO
- ☐ Umbrellas (2)
- ☐ Upside-down sign
- ☐ "Wet Paint"

HUNT FOR HECTOR

WHERE ARE THEY?

Where's Hector?
You'll have to search through these
wacky scenes—and more—to find him!

- Cats at the Dog Mall
- K-9 secret agents
- Fencing dogs at the Olympics
- Fire hydrants in Dogtown
- Bones at the Hall of Fame
- Dancing dogs at school
- Hot dogs in space

. . . and lots more!

Hunt for Hector at the Dog Hall of Fame and...

Hunt for Hector at Dog School and...

- [ ] "Barking King I"
- [ ] Briefcases (3)
- [ ] Canes (2)
- [ ] Cat litter
- [ ] Crown
- [ ] Crying dog
- [ ] "Dog Days"
- [ ] "Doggy Decimal System"
- [ ] "Dog Tail"
- [ ] Easel
- [ ] Empty dog bowls (14)
- [ ] Eraser
- [ ] Fire hydrant
- [ ] Graduation cap
- [ ] Hammer
- [ ] Ladle
- [ ] Man on leash
- [ ] Napkins (2)
- [ ] Paintbrush
- [ ] Pearl necklace
- [ ] Roller skates
- [ ] Ruler
- [ ] Screwdriver
- [ ] Sleeping dog
- [ ] Spoons (3)
- [ ] Stool
- [ ] Straw
- [ ] "Super Dog"
- [ ] Test tubes (4)

Hunt for Hector
among the
Dogcatchers
and...

- ☐ Airplane
- ☐ Barber pole
- ☐ Bathing dog
- ☐ Briefcase
- ☐ Car antenna
- ☐ Cats (5)
- ☐ Convertible car
- ☐ Dog bowls (3)
- ☐ "Dog mail"
- ☐ Dollar signs (11)
- ☐ Empty bowls (2)
- ☐ Fire hose
- ☐ Fire hydrants (4)
- ☐ Fire truck
- ☐ Fishing pole
- ☐ Guitar
- ☐ Heart
- ☐ Manhole
- ☐ Musical note
- ☐ Net
- ☐ Piano
- ☐ Pink hats (8)
- ☐ Rope swing
- ☐ Satellite dish
- ☐ Shower
- ☐ Sirens (2)
- ☐ Tree
- ☐ Turtle
- ☐ "UDS"
- ☐ Umbrella
- ☐ Watermelon
- ☐ Water tower

Hunt for **Hector**
where the
Rich and Famous
Dogs Live
and...

- ☐ Admiral
- ☐ Alligator
- ☐ Artist
- ☐ "Big Wheel"
- ☐ Bird bath
- ☐ Blimp
- ☐ Bone chimney
- ☐ Candle
- ☐ Castle
- ☐ Cat
- ☐ Cooks (2)
- ☐ Crown
- ☐ Dogfish
- ☐ Dog flag
- ☐ Fire hydrant
- ☐ Golfers (2)
- ☐ Guard
- ☐ Heart
- ☐ Heron
- ☐ Human
- ☐ Joggers (3)
- ☐ Periscope
- ☐ Pillow
- ☐ Pool
- ☐ Star
- ☐ Straw
- ☐ Tennis player
- ☐ Umbrella
- ☐ Violinist
- ☐ Water-skier
- ☐ Whale

Hunt for Hector at the K-9 Clean up and...

- ☐ Anchor
- ☐ Bones (2)
- ☐ Broken piggy bank
- ☐ Butterfly net
- ☐ Cane
- ☐ Chimney
- ☐ "Chow" bowl
- ☐ Cowboy hat
- ☐ Doorbell
- ☐ Duck
- ☐ Fake mustache
- ☐ Feather
- ☐ Fire hose
- ☐ Fire hydrants (3)
- ☐ Fishing pole
- ☐ Helicopter
- ☐ "K-9" helmet
- ☐ Manhole cover
- ☐ Motorcycle
- ☐ Pails of water (7)
- ☐ Parachute
- ☐ Penguin
- ☐ Rope ladder
- ☐ Rowboat
- ☐ Sailor's hat
- ☐ Scrub brush
- ☐ Skateboard
- ☐ "S.S. Poseidon"
- ☐ Superpooch
- ☐ Tin cans (4)

Hunt for Hector at the Dog Mall and...

- [ ] Air conditioner
- [ ] Barber's pole
- [ ] Baseball
- [ ] Bone cake
- [ ] "Bone on a Bun"
- [ ] Bookstore
- [ ] Car
- [ ] Cats (2)
- [ ] Chef's hat
- [ ] Clown
- [ ] Cookies (2)
- [ ] Crooked chimney
- [ ] Doghouse
- [ ] Dog in shining armor
- [ ] Fire hydrants (2)
- [ ] "Food Court"
- [ ] "For Rent"
- [ ] Graduate
- [ ] Hockey stick
- [ ] "Hunk" poster
- [ ] Leashes (3)
- [ ] Lollipop
- [ ] Mug
- [ ] Newspaper seller
- [ ] Paper airplane
- [ ] Scissors
- [ ] Spotlight
- [ ] Suitcase
- [ ] Trophy
- [ ] Turkey
- [ ] Witch dog

Hunt for Hector at the Dog Olympics and...

- ☐ Bone bat
- ☐ Bow
- ☐ Bowling ball
- ☐ Broom
- ☐ Bucket
- ☐ Clipboard
- ☐ Diving board
- ☐ Fallen skater
- ☐ Fencing swords (2)
- ☐ Fishing pole
- ☐ Football players (3)
- ☐ Golf tee
- ☐ Hat with propeller
- ☐ Home plate
- ☐ Ice skates (14)
- ☐ Karate dog
- ☐ Ping-pong paddle
- ☐ Pitcher
- ☐ Pole-vaulter
- ☐ Race car
- ☐ Ski jumper
- ☐ Stop sign
- ☐ Target
- ☐ Tennis racket
- ☐ Top hat
- ☐ Trainer
- ☐ TV camera
- ☐ Volleyball
- ☐ Weight lifter
- ☐ Yo-yo

Hunt for Hector at the TV Quiz Show and...

Hunt for Hector
in
Space
and...

- ☐ Bench
- ☐ Blimp
- ☐ Boat
- ☐ Bone antenna
- ☐ Bone smokestack
- ☐ Boxing glove
- ☐ Bus
- ☐ Cars (3)
- ☐ Diving board
- ☐ "Dog fish"
- ☐ Dog in trash can
- ☐ "Dog paddle"
- ☐ Earth
- ☐ Emergency dog
- ☐ Graduate dog
- ☐ Heart with arrow
- ☐ Hot dog
- ☐ Juggler
- ☐ Mailbag
- ☐ Nut
- ☐ Old tire
- ☐ Pirate
- ☐ Pizza
- ☐ Pluto
- ☐ Pup in a cup
- ☐ Roller-coaster
- ☐ Space map
- ☐ Star with tail
- ☐ Top hat
- ☐ UFO
- ☐ Unicycle
- ☐ Vampire Dog

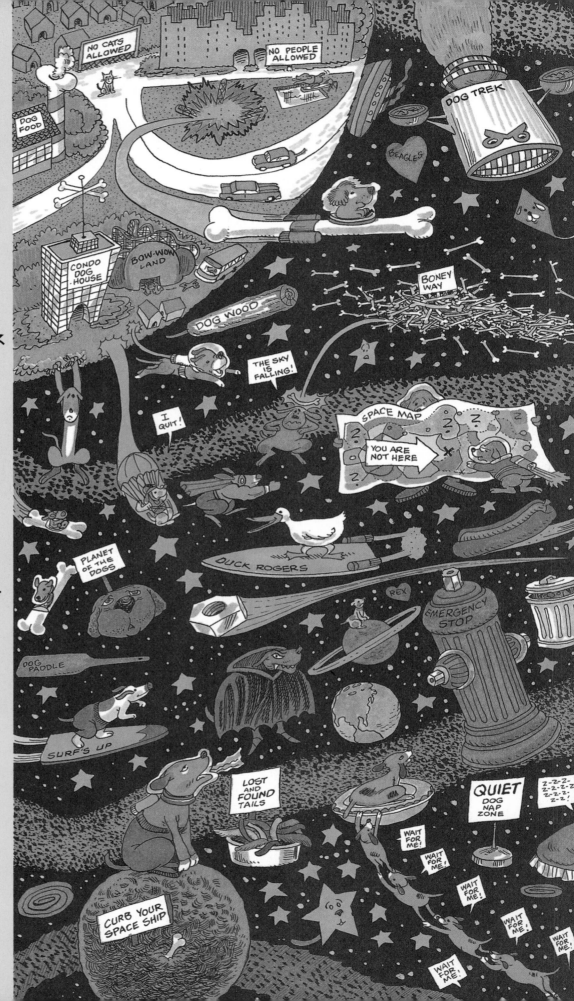

Hunt for Hector
in
Dogtown
and...

- [ ] Baby carriage
- [ ] Barbecue
- [ ] "Bark Your Horn"
- [ ] Basketball
- [ ] Bicycle
- [ ] Birds (2)
- [ ] Boat
- [ ] Crossing guard
- [ ] "Dog cookies"
- [ ] Dog fountain
- [ ] Falling "G"
- [ ] Gas pump
- [ ] Hammer
- [ ] Hard hats (3)
- [ ] Human on leash
- [ ] Lawn mower
- [ ] Mailbox
- [ ] Manhole
- [ ] Piano
- [ ] Pool
- [ ] Sailor
- [ ] Santa Claus
- [ ] Screwdriver
- [ ] Skateboard
- [ ] Soccer ball
- [ ] Sock
- [ ] Streetlight
- [ ] Super Dog
- [ ] Swimming pool
- [ ] Trash cans (2)
- [ ] TV
- [ ] Wrench

HUNT FOR HECTOR SEARCH FOR SAM FIND FREDDIE LOOK FOR LISA

LOOK FOR LISA

WHERE ARE THEY?

Look for Lisa in all sorts of crazy places!
While you're looking,
you'll see crazy things, such as:

- ◎ Hippos at a rock concert
- ◎ Cactuses on the beach
- ◎ Parrots in the library
- ◎ Surfers on a farm
- ◎ Frogs at the flea market
- ◎ Snow White at the marathon
- ◎ Unicorns in Utah

. . . and much, much more!

Look for **Lisa** at the **Marathon** and...

- ☐ Angel
- ☐ Barrel
- ☐ Basketball
- ☐ Bucket
- ☐ Cane
- ☐ Chef
- ☐ Cowboy
- ☐ Deer
- ☐ Diving board
- ☐ Doctor
- ☐ Elephants (2)
- ☐ Ice-cream cone
- ☐ Kite
- ☐ Motorcycle
- ☐ Musical notes (3)
- ☐ Net
- ☐ Octopus
- ☐ Periscope
- ☐ Policeman
- ☐ Rocket
- ☐ Roller skates
- ☐ Sad face
- ☐ Scooter
- ☐ "Shortcut"
- ☐ Sombrero
- ☐ Speed skater
- ☐ Spotted dog
- ☐ Strongman
- ☐ Surfer
- ☐ Taxi
- ☐ Tuba
- ☐ Umbrella

Look for Lisa
After School
and...

- [ ] Balloon
- [ ] Basketballs (2)
- [ ] Baton
- [ ] Bird
- [ ] Camera
- [ ] Chimney
- [ ] Clock faces (2)
- [ ] Donkey
- [ ] Elephant
- [ ] Fish with a hat
- [ ] Flower
- [ ] Grocery cart
- [ ] Hat with propeller
- [ ] Huck Finn
- [ ] Igloo
- [ ] Paper hat
- [ ] Parrot
- [ ] Pencil
- [ ] Pig
- [ ] Plane
- [ ] Rabbit
- [ ] Robot
- [ ] Sailor
- [ ] Ski jumper
- [ ] Smelly potion
- [ ] Snowman
- [ ] Stool
- [ ] Sunglasses
- [ ] Turtle
- [ ] Unicorn
- [ ] Viking helmet

Look for **Lisa** at the **Rock Concert** and...

- ☐ Alien
- ☐ Balloons (6)
- ☐ Barbell
- ☐ Bowling ball
- ☐ Crown
- ☐ Doctor
- ☐ Fish tank
- ☐ Flamingo
- ☐ Flowers
- ☐ Hot-dog stand
- ☐ Knight
- ☐ Lamppost
- ☐ Masked man
- ☐ Moon
- ☐ Mummy
- ☐ Net
- ☐ Painter
- ☐ Prisoner
- ☐ Rabbit
- ☐ Snowman
- ☐ Stack of pizza boxes
- ☐ Stars (6)
- ☐ Tin man
- ☐ Tombstones (2)
- ☐ Trampoline
- ☐ Viking
- ☐ Waiter
- ☐ Witch
- ☐ Zebra

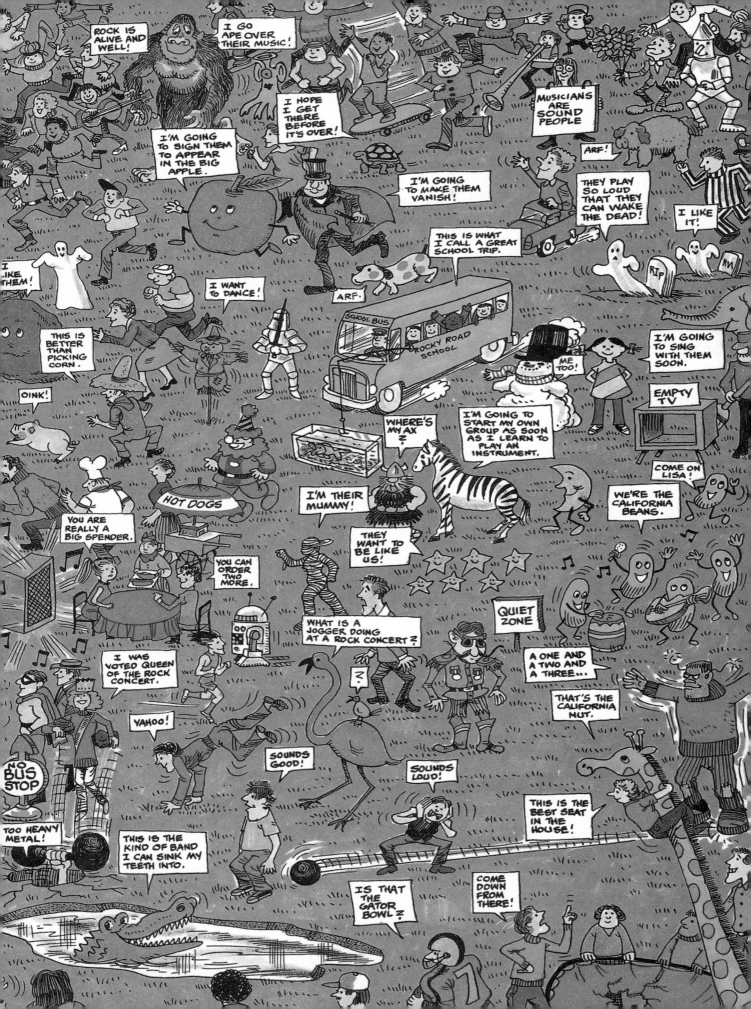

Look for **Lisa** on the **Farm** and...

- ☐ Cactus
- ☐ Cave
- ☐ Clouds (3)
- ☐ Donkey
- ☐ "Don't Stop" sign
- ☐ Egg
- ☐ Elephant
- ☐ Eskimo
- ☐ Finish line
- ☐ Fox
- ☐ Ghost
- ☐ Giant pumpkin
- ☐ "Grade A"
- ☐ Horses (3)
- ☐ Lion
- ☐ Log pile
- ☐ Message in a bottle
- ☐ Net
- ☐ Periscope
- ☐ Pitchfork
- ☐ Policeman
- ☐ Prisoner
- ☐ Rowboat
- ☐ Scuba diver
- ☐ Stop sign
- ☐ "Summer"
- ☐ Surfboards (2)
- ☐ Tent
- ☐ Turkey
- ☐ Water bucket
- ☐ Weather vane

Look for **Lisa** at the **Beach** and...

- ☐ Artist
- ☐ Beach ball
- ☐ Broom
- ☐ Bunch of balloons
- ☐ Cactus (4)
- ☐ Castle
- ☐ Cello
- ☐ Crocodile
- ☐ Cruise ship
- ☐ Diving board
- ☐ Hearts (3)
- ☐ Horse
- ☐ Jack-in-the-box
- ☐ Kite
- ☐ Lifeguard
- ☐ Lost swim trunks
- ☐ Magnifying glass
- ☐ Merman
- ☐ Palm trees (3)
- ☐ Pickle barrel
- ☐ Policeman
- ☐ Sailboat
- ☐ Sailors (2)
- ☐ Sea serpent
- ☐ Seahorse
- ☐ Starfish (9)
- ☐ Swans (2)
- ☐ Telescope
- ☐ Trash can
- ☐ Tricycle
- ☐ Turtle
- ☐ Whale

Look for **Lisa** at the **Big Sale** and...

- ☐ Balloon
- ☐ Clothespins (9)
- ☐ Count Dracula
- ☐ Disappearing men (2)
- ☐ "Don't Stop Shopping"
- ☐ Flower hat
- ☐ Football
- ☐ Football helmet
- ☐ Gumball machine
- ☐ Hard hat
- ☐ Janitor
- ☐ Kite
- ☐ Magic mirror
- ☐ Manhole cover
- ☐ Octopus
- ☐ Paint can
- ☐ Paper airplane
- ☐ Pig
- ☐ Pogo stick
- ☐ Polka-dot shorts
- ☐ Rabbit
- ☐ Rain slicker
- ☐ Rat
- ☐ Robot
- ☐ Roller skates
- ☐ Shirtless shopper
- ☐ Ski jump
- ☐ Skis (8)
- ☐ Teddy bear
- ☐ Turtle

Look for **Lisa** in the
Ocean
and...

- [ ] Baby
- [ ] Barrel
- [ ] Baseball bat
- [ ] Basketball
- [ ] Boot
- [ ] Bucket
- [ ] Captain's hat
- [ ] Elephant
- [ ] Fish (3)
- [ ] Guitar
- [ ] Harp
- [ ] Heart
- [ ] Homework
- [ ] Hot-air balloon
- [ ] Ice-cream cone
- [ ] Key
- [ ] Oars (5)
- [ ] Painting
- [ ] Palm tree
- [ ] Scuba diver
- [ ] Shark fins (2)
- [ ] Slice of watermelon
- [ ] Sock
- [ ] Surfer
- [ ] Television
- [ ] Tin can
- [ ] Tire
- [ ] Tree

Look for **Lisa** at the **Library** and...

- [ ] Baseball
- [ ] Birdcage
- [ ] Bowling pins (10)
- [ ] Brooms (2)
- [ ] Cactus
- [ ] Cactus book
- [ ] Cake
- [ ] Campfire
- [ ] Candle
- [ ] Car
- [ ] Football player
- [ ] Frying pan
- [ ] Globe
- [ ] Hamburger
- [ ] Hearts (4)
- [ ] Hockey stick
- [ ] Hot dog
- [ ] Jack-in-the-box
- [ ] Knight
- [ ] Monster hands (3)
- [ ] Musical note
- [ ] Napoleon
- [ ] Old tire
- [ ] Pole-vaulter
- [ ] Policewoman
- [ ] "Quiet" signs (6)
- [ ] Smiley face
- [ ] Teapot
- [ ] Trapdoor
- [ ] Tricycle
- [ ] Wagon
- [ ] Witch

Look for **Lisa** at the
Amusement Park
and...

- ☐ All-north weather vane
- ☐ Archer
- ☐ Cheese
- ☐ Clock
- ☐ Clowns (3)
- ☐ Cowboys (2)
- ☐ Crocodile
- ☐ Crooked chimney
- ☐ Diving board
- ☐ Dollar sign
- ☐ Fishing pole
- ☐ Heads without bodies (2)
- ☐ Ice block
- ☐ Manhole
- ☐ Moon
- ☐ Mousehole
- ☐ Mummy
- ☐ Pear
- ☐ Snowman
- ☐ Space explorer
- ☐ Tent
- ☐ Tied-up man
- ☐ Tin man
- ☐ Tombstones (3)
- ☐ "Tunnel of Love"
- ☐ Umbrella
- ☐ Witch
- ☐ Wristwatches (7)

Look for Lisa at the Flea Market and...

- ☐ Birdcages (2)
- ☐ Clown doll
- ☐ Court jester
- ☐ Cowboy hat
- ☐ Crown
- ☐ Elephant
- ☐ Elf
- ☐ Fish (3)
- ☐ Fishing hook
- ☐ "Flea Market Map"
- ☐ Football
- ☐ Golf club
- ☐ Graduate
- ☐ Horse
- ☐ Monster hand
- ☐ Necklace
- ☐ Old tire
- ☐ Paintbrush
- ☐ Pear
- ☐ Records (8)
- ☐ Saddle
- ☐ Sailor hat
- ☐ Scuba diver
- ☐ Shopping bag
- ☐ Skateboard
- ☐ Telephone booth
- ☐ Train conductor
- ☐ Trumpet
- ☐ Wheelbarrow
- ☐ Witch

Look for **Lisa** as the **Circus Comes to Town** and...

- ☐ Aliens (2)
- ☐ Barbell
- ☐ Bass drum
- ☐ Bone
- ☐ Broom
- ☐ Camel
- ☐ Cowboys (4)
- ☐ Crown
- ☐ "Enter"
- ☐ Flags (7)
- ☐ Frankenstein's monster
- ☐ Hole
- ☐ Juggler
- ☐ Musical notes (2)
- ☐ Net
- ☐ Plates (7)
- ☐ Police officers (2)
- ☐ Poodle
- ☐ Rabbit
- ☐ Sad face
- ☐ Soldiers (2)
- ☐ Stroller
- ☐ Tin man
- ☐ Turtle
- ☐ Unicorn
- ☐ Unicycle
- ☐ Whistle
- ☐ Witch

LOOK FOR LISA　　FIND FREDDIE　　SEARCH FOR SAM　　HUNT FOR HECTOR

SEARCH FOR SAM

WHERE ARE THEY?

Sam's a sly cat, so good luck in your search!
You'll encounter hilarious characters in strange
scenes as you search for Sam.

- Dogs at the cat show
- Rhinos at the disco
- Alley cats in ancient Egypt
- Meows at midnight
- Fat cats at the gym
- Sharks in Cat City
- Dogbusters

. . . and lots more!

Search for Sam
in
Cat City
and...

- [ ] Airplane
- [ ] Antenna
- [ ] Balloons (2)
- [ ] Barrel
- [ ] Blimp
- [ ] Candle
- [ ] Cracked window
- [ ] Elephant
- [ ] Fire hydrant
- [ ] Flowerpot
- [ ] Fur coat
- [ ] Hammer
- [ ] Hard hats (3)
- [ ] Mailbox
- [ ] Manhole cover
- [ ] Motorcycle
- [ ] Musical notes (8)
- [ ] Octopus
- [ ] Piano
- [ ] Red bow
- [ ] Rocket
- [ ] Rooster
- [ ] Scarf
- [ ] Sharks (3)
- [ ] Shovel
- [ ] Sock
- [ ] Sun
- [ ] Telephone booth
- [ ] Toolbox
- [ ] Towel
- [ ] Turtle
- [ ] Waiter

Search for Sam
at
Fat Cat Gym
and...

- ☐ Book
- ☐ Bowling ball
- ☐ Breaking rope
- ☐ Burned feet
- ☐ Cat food dish
- ☐ Catnap
- ☐ Clipboard
- ☐ Cool cat
- ☐ Dog bone
- ☐ "Do Not Touch"
- ☐ Escaped bird
- ☐ Fish (2)
- ☐ Fishbowl
- ☐ Fish skeletons (6)
- ☐ Hearts (3)
- ☐ Helmet
- ☐ Ice-cream cones (2)
- ☐ Jump rope
- ☐ Money
- ☐ Pair of boxing gloves
- ☐ Pizza
- ☐ Prisoner
- ☐ Punching bags (2)
- ☐ Rats (3)
- ☐ Stationary bike
- ☐ Sweat bands (13)
- ☐ Tail warmer
- ☐ Torn pants
- ☐ Window
- ☐ Yoga mats (3)

Search for Sam at the
Midnight Meowing
and...

- ☐ Baseball
- ☐ Baseball bat
- ☐ Birdhouse
- ☐ Can
- ☐ Cannon
- ☐ Cloud
- ☐ Egg
- ☐ Fishbowl
- ☐ Fish skeletons (2)
- ☐ Football
- ☐ Gate
- ☐ Jack-o'-lantern
- ☐ Light
- ☐ Microphone
- ☐ Moon
- ☐ "No Welcome" mat
- ☐ Old tire
- ☐ Piggy bank
- ☐ Police car
- ☐ Policeman
- ☐ Pot
- ☐ Record player
- ☐ Rolling pin
- ☐ Spoon
- ☐ Stacks of paper (2)
- ☐ Stars (4)
- ☐ Table
- ☐ Tent
- ☐ UFO
- ☐ Wood planks (3)
- ☐ Yo-yo

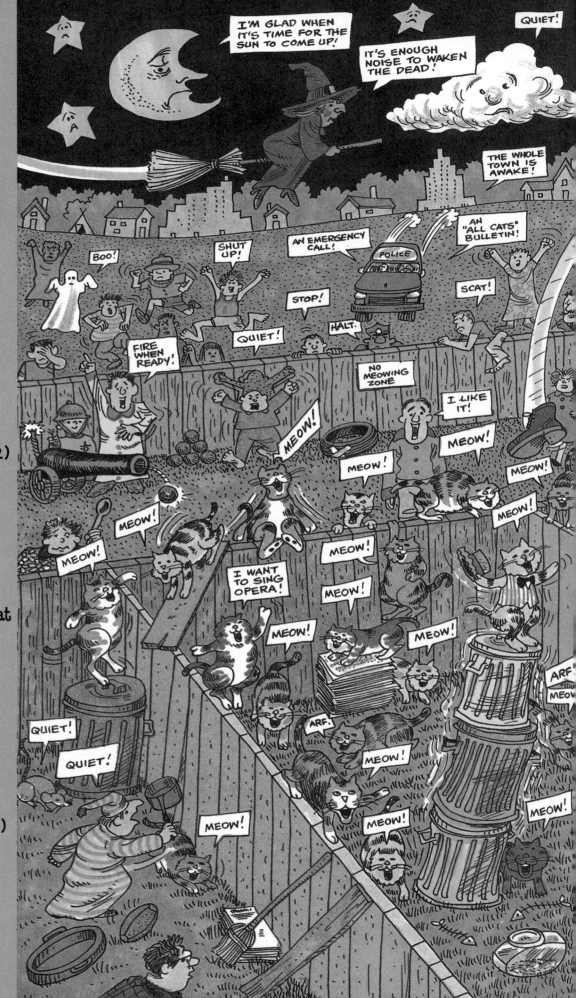

Search for Sam
at the
Disco
and...

- ☐ Ballerina
- ☐ Blue rhinos (2)
- ☐ Breakdance cat
- ☐ Cat blowing horn
- ☐ Chef
- ☐ Clipboard
- ☐ Clown cat
- ☐ Cowboy cat
- ☐ Disco ball
- ☐ Doctor
- ☐ Dog
- ☐ Duck
- ☐ Earplug seller
- ☐ Earrings
- ☐ Eye patch
- ☐ Flowerpot
- ☐ Hard hat
- ☐ Karate cat
- ☐ Lampshade
- ☐ Pig
- ☐ Pirate sword
- ☐ Pizza
- ☐ Police officer
- ☐ Record player
- ☐ Roller skates
- ☐ Skis
- ☐ Snow cat
- ☐ Speakers (10)
- ☐ Sunglasses
- ☐ Swinging cat
- ☐ Top hat
- ☐ Wooden leg

Search for Sam in Ancient Egypt and...

- ☐ Antenna
- ☐ Arrows (4)
- ☐ Boats (2)
- ☐ Boxes (3)
- ☐ Bucket
- ☐ Cats in bikinis (2)
- ☐ Falling coconuts (2)
- ☐ Fan
- ☐ Fire
- ☐ Fishing poles (2)
- ☐ Flying carpet
- ☐ Guard cats (5)
- ☐ Hippo
- ☐ Horse
- ☐ Jester
- ☐ Mummies (2)
- ☐ Palm trees (2)
- ☐ Pyramids (8)
- ☐ Quicksand
- ☐ Red birds (4)
- ☐ Red bow
- ☐ Rolled paper
- ☐ Sand pail
- ☐ Shovel
- ☐ Smiley face
- ☐ Snakes (2)
- ☐ Snowman
- ☐ Taxi
- ☐ Telephone
- ☐ Umbrella

Search for **Sam** at the **Cat Show** and...

- ☐ Ball of yarn
- ☐ Banjo
- ☐ Beach chair
- ☐ Bib
- ☐ Bones (2)
- ☐ Broom
- ☐ Camera
- ☐ Coconuts (2)
- ☐ Cow
- ☐ Cracked wall
- ☐ Cymbals (2)
- ☐ Fish bones (4)
- ☐ Fishing pole
- ☐ Graduate
- ☐ Guitar
- ☐ Hearts (3)
- ☐ Joggers (2)
- ☐ Lion
- ☐ Man in a cat suit
- ☐ Net
- ☐ Newspaper
- ☐ Palm tree
- ☐ Pizza boxes (2)
- ☐ Pool
- ☐ Scarf
- ☐ Sombrero
- ☐ Red bow
- ☐ Red curtain
- ☐ Royal cat
- ☐ Ticket booth
- ☐ Tombstone
- ☐ Witch

Search for **Sam** with the **Dogbusters** and...

- ☐ Balloon
- ☐ Birdhouse
- ☐ Bones (13)
- ☐ Bridge
- ☐ Broom
- ☐ Clown
- ☐ Crane
- ☐ Crocodile
- ☐ Detective
- ☐ Dogs in tree (2)
- ☐ Fish (4)
- ☐ Flag
- ☐ Flower
- ☐ Hollow log
- ☐ Horse
- ☐ Jack-o'-lantern
- ☐ Ladders (3)
- ☐ Lamppost
- ☐ Manhole cover
- ☐ Old tire
- ☐ Pizza box
- ☐ Saddle
- ☐ Sailboat
- ☐ Siren
- ☐ Surfboard
- ☐ Taxi
- ☐ Tent
- ☐ Tightrope walker
- ☐ Turtle
- ☐ Umbrella
- ☐ Wanted poster
- ☐ Witch

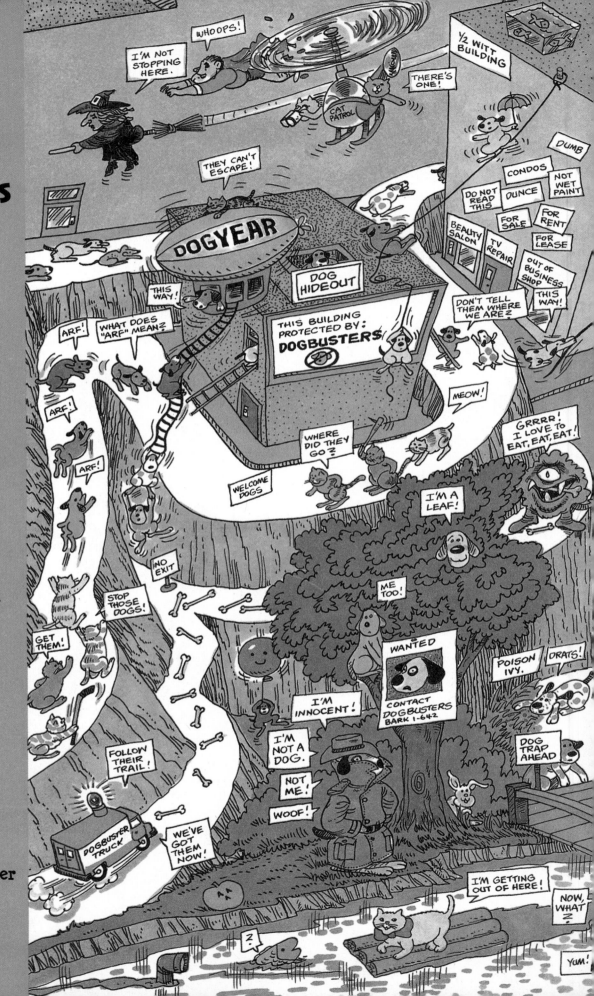

Search for **Sam** at the **North Pole** and...

- ☐ Badge
- ☐ Bells (2)
- ☐ Bread
- ☐ Broken chair
- ☐ Cactus
- ☐ Campfire
- ☐ Chef's hat
- ☐ Clock
- ☐ Fish
- ☐ Fishing pole
- ☐ Football
- ☐ Globe
- ☐ Green sock
- ☐ Hammer
- ☐ Kite
- ☐ Locomotive
- ☐ Miner's hat
- ☐ Musical notes (3)
- ☐ Ornament
- ☐ Pizza
- ☐ Polar bear
- ☐ Reindeer
- ☐ Satellite dish
- ☐ Singing birds (2)
- ☐ Skier
- ☐ Snake with a hat
- ☐ Stepladder
- ☐ Toy car
- ☐ Yo-yo
- ☐ Zebras (2)

SEARCH FOR SAM

FIND FREDDIE

HUNT FOR HECTOR

LOOK FOR LISA

DETECT DONALD

Detect Donald
in the
Middle Ages
and...

- [ ] Animal horns (2)
- [ ] Axe
- [ ] Baseball caps (2)
- [ ] Bird
- [ ] Candles (3)
- [ ] Clothespin
- [ ] Crutch
- [ ] Donkey
- [ ] Dragon
- [ ] Duck
- [ ] Fan
- [ ] Fish
- [ ] Flags (5)
- [ ] Hat feathers (4)
- [ ] Helmet with horns
- [ ] Lances (3)
- [ ] Mouse
- [ ] Propeller
- [ ] Queen
- [ ] Red bows (2)
- [ ] Sergeant's stripes
- [ ] Stars (2)
- [ ] Sunglasses (2)
- [ ] Tombstone
- [ ] UFO
- [ ] Weather vane

Detect Donald
in
Cartoonland
and...

- ☐ Banana peel
- ☐ Baseball bats (2)
- ☐ Bees (4)
- ☐ Broom
- ☐ Burst balloon
- ☐ Chicken
- ☐ Crow
- ☐ Elephants (2)
- ☐ Elf
- ☐ Firefighter
- ☐ Flower
- ☐ Gingerbread man
- ☐ Golf tee
- ☐ Horses (2)
- ☐ Hot dog
- ☐ Lamp
- ☐ Masks (2)
- ☐ Mushroom
- ☐ Pie
- ☐ Pirate hat
- ☐ Pot
- ☐ Rabbit
- ☐ Sandwich
- ☐ Saxophone
- ☐ Scarf
- ☐ Snake
- ☐ Swiss cheese
- ☐ Underwear

Detect Donald at the **Pirates' Battle** and...

- ☐ Arrows (2)
- ☐ Banana peel
- ☐ Basket
- ☐ Buckets (2)
- ☐ Dog
- ☐ Dollar sign
- ☐ Eye patches (4)
- ☐ Falling boots (2)
- ☐ Fire hydrant
- ☐ Flowerpot
- ☐ Football
- ☐ Ladder
- ☐ Mask
- ☐ Milk carton
- ☐ Moon
- ☐ Musical note
- ☐ Paper hat
- ☐ Peanut seller
- ☐ Pointed hat
- ☐ Rabbit
- ☐ Red bows (4)
- ☐ Sailboat
- ☐ Shovel
- ☐ Snake
- ☐ Stools (2)
- ☐ Striped shirt
- ☐ Telescopes (2)

Detect Donald
in
Napoleon's France
and...

- ☐ Alien
- ☐ Arrow
- ☐ Basket
- ☐ Basketball players (2)
- ☐ Baton twirler
- ☐ Bear
- ☐ Bowling ball
- ☐ Crown
- ☐ Fishing pole
- ☐ French bread
- ☐ Garbage can
- ☐ Haystack
- ☐ Ice-cream cone
- ☐ Jack-o'-lantern
- ☐ Key
- ☐ Lost boot
- ☐ Mask
- ☐ Mermaid
- ☐ Mouse
- ☐ Net
- ☐ Paintbrush
- ☐ Propeller
- ☐ Red bird
- ☐ Rooster
- ☐ Skull
- ☐ Tin can
- ☐ Turtle
- ☐ Watering can
- ☐ Witch

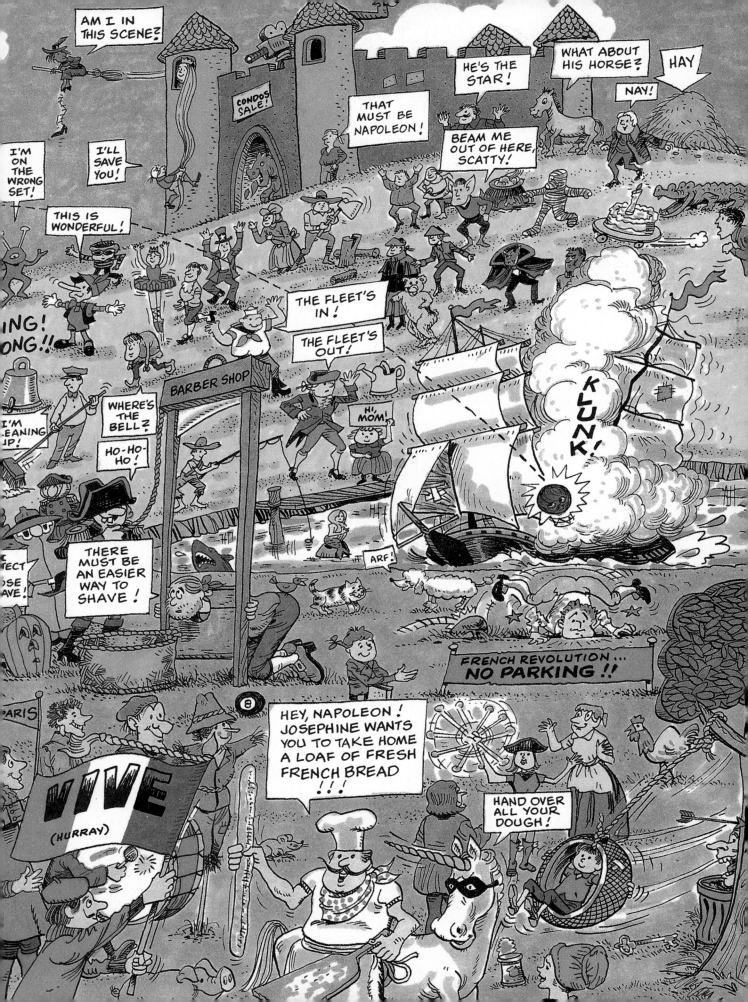

Detect Donald
in
Ancient Rome
and...

- [ ] Arrow
- [ ] Backwards helmet
- [ ] Balloon
- [ ] Cactus
- [ ] Caesar
- [ ] Cat
- [ ] Falling rock
- [ ] Flower
- [ ] Horseless chariot
- [ ] Jack-o'-lantern
- [ ] Julius and Augustus
- [ ] Kite
- [ ] Mask
- [ ] Painted egg
- [ ] Pig
- [ ] Pizza box
- [ ] Puddles (2)
- [ ] Rabbit
- [ ] Shield
- [ ] Skull
- [ ] Slice of pizza
- [ ] Snake
- [ ] Sock
- [ ] Spears (2)
- [ ] Star
- [ ] Underwear

Detect Donald
in
Prehistoric Times
and...

- ☐ Blue hats (3)
- ☐ Briefcase
- ☐ Broom
- ☐ Car
- ☐ Cave
- ☐ Crown
- ☐ Football
- ☐ Glass pitcher
- ☐ Guitar
- ☐ Kite
- ☐ Lasso
- ☐ Lion
- ☐ Logs (2)
- ☐ Lunch box
- ☐ Periscope
- ☐ Pig
- ☐ Pink flamingo
- ☐ Red bows (4)
- ☐ Snakes (3)
- ☐ Soccer ball
- ☐ Spoon
- ☐ Stone axe
- ☐ Superhero
- ☐ Tin man
- ☐ Tire
- ☐ Trumpet
- ☐ Volcano

Detect Donald at the Academy Awards and...

- ☐ Bow ties (2)
- ☐ Candle
- ☐ Cup
- ☐ Dinosaurs (3)
- ☐ Dracula
- ☐ Duck
- ☐ Envelope
- ☐ Eye patch
- ☐ Flying bat
- ☐ Fork
- ☐ George Washington
- ☐ Handkerchief
- ☐ Helmets (3)
- ☐ Medal
- ☐ Necktie
- ☐ Painted egg
- ☐ Rat
- ☐ Red beret
- ☐ Rose
- ☐ Saw
- ☐ Sleeping man
- ☐ Soldier
- ☐ Spear
- ☐ Spoon
- ☐ Target
- ☐ Wooden leg

LOOK FOR LAURA   DETECT DONALD   FIND FRANKIE   SEARCH FOR SUSIE

FIND FRANKIE

Find Frankie at the Monster Club Meeting and...

- [ ] Bow ties (3)
- [ ] Cane
- [ ] Cracked mirror
- [ ] Eyeglasses
- [ ] Jack-o'-lantern
- [ ] Knight in armor
- [ ] Mouseholes (2)
- [ ] Mummy
- [ ] Neckties (4)
- [ ] Parrot
- [ ] Pirate
- [ ] Propeller
- [ ] Rain boots
- [ ] Scar
- [ ] Shelves (2)
- [ ] Ski hat
- [ ] Smelly monster
- [ ] Snake
- [ ] Straw
- [ ] Suspenders
- [ ] Television
- [ ] Towel
- [ ] Turtle
- [ ] Witch
- [ ] Wooden club
- [ ] Yo-yo

Find Frankie on the **Street** and...

- [ ] Benches (2)
- [ ] Books (2)
- [ ] Candle
- [ ] Clowns (2)
- [ ] Crayon
- [ ] Crowns (2)
- [ ] Dogs (2)
- [ ] Dripping faucet
- [ ] Duck
- [ ] Fish
- [ ] Flower hat
- [ ] Flowerpots (2)
- [ ] Handbag
- [ ] Hard hat
- [ ] Jogger
- [ ] Mouse ears
- [ ] Newspaper
- [ ] Parrot
- [ ] Peanut
- [ ] Pinocchio
- [ ] Postal worker
- [ ] Sailor hats (2)
- [ ] Sombrero
- [ ] Spaceman
- [ ] Suspenders (3 sets)
- [ ] Tepee
- [ ] Toolbox
- [ ] Umbrella
- [ ] Watering can

Find Frankie at the **Theater** and...

- ☐ Ballerina
- ☐ Baseball cap
- ☐ Beard
- ☐ Boat
- ☐ Candy cane
- ☐ Cane
- ☐ Cannon
- ☐ Cowboys (2)
- ☐ Fire hydrant
- ☐ Flying shoe
- ☐ Gorilla
- ☐ Graduation cap
- ☐ Helmet with horns (2)
- ☐ High-top sneaker
- ☐ Hot dog
- ☐ Ladders (2)
- ☐ Man in the moon
- ☐ Owl
- ☐ Paper airplane
- ☐ Propeller
- ☐ Scar
- ☐ Sheep
- ☐ Skull
- ☐ Suspenders (2 pairs)
- ☐ Target
- ☐ Tent
- ☐ Trapeze artist
- ☐ Underwear

Find Frankie at the **Zoo** and...

- [ ] Alligator
- [ ] Artist
- [ ] Blue hats (3)
- [ ] Bucket
- [ ] Carrots (2)
- [ ] Clothesline
- [ ] Fishing pole
- [ ] Half-moon
- [ ] Jack-o'-lantern
- [ ] Kids on fathers' shoulders (2)
- [ ] Kneepads
- [ ] Ladder
- [ ] Matador
- [ ] Orange birds (2)
- [ ] Park bench
- [ ] Periscope
- [ ] Pink flamingo
- [ ] Purple hats (3)
- [ ] Purple sock
- [ ] Rabbits (2)
- [ ] Red bandannas (2)
- [ ] Red hats (4)
- [ ] Stool
- [ ] Strollers (2)
- [ ] Tiger
- [ ] Umbrella
- [ ] Zookeepers (3)

Find Frankie at the Aquarium and...

- ☐ Backpack
- ☐ Bottle
- ☐ Camera
- ☐ Cowboy
- ☐ Doghouses (2)
- ☐ Electric eel
- ☐ Faucet
- ☐ Ghost
- ☐ Green handbag
- ☐ Guitar
- ☐ Lamp
- ☐ Mushroom
- ☐ Net
- ☐ Robot
- ☐ Rocking horse
- ☐ Rowboat
- ☐ Sailboat
- ☐ Sailor hat
- ☐ Scooter
- ☐ Snorkel & mask
- ☐ Snowman
- ☐ Snowshoes
- ☐ Starfish (3)
- ☐ Swords (2)
- ☐ Teacher
- ☐ Telescope
- ☐ Tin man
- ☐ Turtles (3)
- ☐ Whip
- ☐ Witch
- ☐ Wooden bucket

Find Frankie in the **Arcade** and...

- ☐ Balloon
- ☐ Baseball
- ☐ Beach ball
- ☐ Bees (2)
- ☐ Birdcage
- ☐ Black cat
- ☐ Book
- ☐ Bucket
- ☐ Cannon
- ☐ Dracula
- ☐ Faucet
- ☐ Football
- ☐ Hard hat
- ☐ Jack-o'-lantern
- ☐ Lightning
- ☐ Maze
- ☐ Mouse
- ☐ Mummy
- ☐ Policeman
- ☐ Rocket
- ☐ Sailor hat
- ☐ Stuffed animal
- ☐ Sunglasses
- ☐ Target
- ☐ Top hat
- ☐ Turtle
- ☐ Umbrella
- ☐ Yo-yo

Find Frankie in the **Suburbs** and...

- ☐ Basketball
- ☐ Bone
- ☐ Books (3)
- ☐ Broken window
- ☐ Broom
- ☐ "Dead End"
- ☐ Flying bat
- ☐ Gate
- ☐ Ghost
- ☐ Golf bag
- ☐ Guitar
- ☐ Hammock
- ☐ Haunted house
- ☐ Jogger
- ☐ Jump rope
- ☐ Mailbox
- ☐ Mail delivery
- ☐ Monster hands (2)
- ☐ Mouse
- ☐ Rabbit
- ☐ Shovel
- ☐ Snake
- ☐ Sunglasses
- ☐ Superhero
- ☐ Tea bag
- ☐ Tire swing
- ☐ Trash cans (3)
- ☐ Tuba
- ☐ TV antenna

Find Frankie at the **Monsters' New Clubhouse** and...

- ☐ "13" (4)
- ☐ Bee
- ☐ Broom
- ☐ Candles (2)
- ☐ Clouds (2)
- ☐ Cobweb
- ☐ Doormat
- ☐ Flower
- ☐ Football
- ☐ Heart
- ☐ Light bulb
- ☐ Mousehole
- ☐ Mustache
- ☐ Neckties (2)
- ☐ Octopus
- ☐ Pirate
- ☐ Pointed hats (2)
- ☐ Sled
- ☐ Smiling ghosts (2)
- ☐ Smiling star
- ☐ Snake
- ☐ Tic-tac-toe
- ☐ Tiny monster
- ☐ Trapdoor
- ☐ Trees (2)
- ☐ Turtle
- ☐ Umbrella
- ☐ Unhappy moon

FIND FRANKIE   SEARCH FOR SUSIE   LOOK FOR LAURA   DETECT DONALD

LOOK FOR LAURA

Look for Laura in the **Ocean** and...

- ☐ Baseball bat
- ☐ Bell
- ☐ Birdhouse
- ☐ Bottle
- ☐ Cheese
- ☐ Crown
- ☐ Duck
- ☐ Empty turtle shell
- ☐ Fishhook
- ☐ Flowerpot
- ☐ Football
- ☐ Graduation cap
- ☐ Key
- ☐ Life preserver
- ☐ Lollipop
- ☐ Milk carton
- ☐ Net
- ☐ Octopus
- ☐ Old boot
- ☐ Pear
- ☐ Pointed hat
- ☐ Pot
- ☐ Sailboat
- ☐ Screwdriver
- ☐ Sea horse
- ☐ Snorkel & mask
- ☐ Starfish
- ☐ Sword

Look for **Laura** at the **Watering Hole** and...

- ☐ Baby bird
- ☐ Birdcage
- ☐ Briefcase
- ☐ Clothespins (2)
- ☐ Coconuts (4)
- ☐ Donkey
- ☐ Duck
- ☐ Feather
- ☐ Fish (3)
- ☐ Giraffe
- ☐ Headband
- ☐ Heart
- ☐ Hippo
- ☐ Leopard
- ☐ Lions (2)
- ☐ Log
- ☐ Lollipop
- ☐ Octopus
- ☐ Ping-pong paddle
- ☐ Radio
- ☐ Rhinoceros
- ☐ Robot
- ☐ Snake
- ☐ Turtle
- ☐ TV set
- ☐ Worm

Look for **Laura** at the
Bah-ha Bazaar
and...

- [ ] Beach ball
- [ ] Broom
- [ ] Cat
- [ ] Clouds (2)
- [ ] Coconuts (4)
- [ ] Donkey
- [ ] Elephant
- [ ] Flying carpets (2)
- [ ] Football
- [ ] Genie
- [ ] Horn
- [ ] Ice-cream cone
- [ ] Igloo
- [ ] Kite
- [ ] Necklace
- [ ] Oil well
- [ ] Pillow fight
- [ ] Rabbit
- [ ] Shovel
- [ ] Skier
- [ ] Snail
- [ ] Snakes (4)
- [ ] Straw baskets (2)
- [ ] Sunglasses
- [ ] Telescope
- [ ] Tents (4)

Look for **Laura** in **Europe** and...

- ☐ Backpacks (2)
- ☐ Basket
- ☐ Bear
- ☐ "Black Sea"
- ☐ Book
- ☐ Bus
- ☐ Cars (2)
- ☐ Castle
- ☐ Cowboy hat
- ☐ Crown
- ☐ Dog
- ☐ Eyeglasses
- ☐ Fishing pole
- ☐ Ghost
- ☐ Greek ruin
- ☐ Head scarf
- ☐ Hot-air balloon
- ☐ Knight
- ☐ Maps (2)
- ☐ Moose
- ☐ Mountain climber
- ☐ Sailboat
- ☐ Scarves (2)
- ☐ Sleigh
- ☐ Suitcase
- ☐ Tunnel
- ☐ Windmill
- ☐ Yellow bird

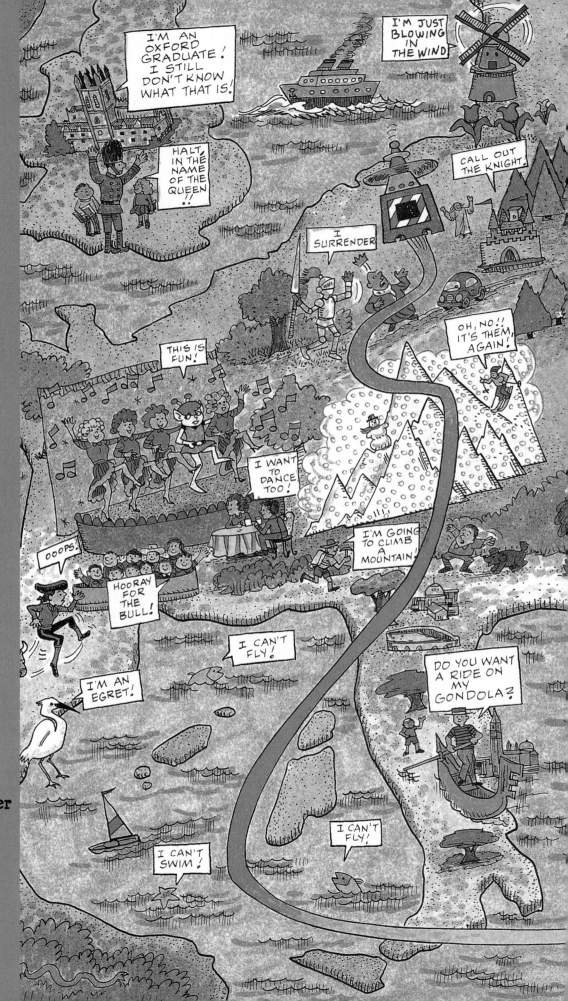

Look for Laura at the Circus and...

- [ ] Bandannas (2)
- [ ] Bicycle
- [ ] Bird
- [ ] Broom
- [ ] Car
- [ ] Cat
- [ ] Crown
- [ ] Drum
- [ ] Earmuff
- [ ] Flowerpot
- [ ] Flying shoe
- [ ] Football helmet
- [ ] Giraffe
- [ ] Lamp
- [ ] Mustaches (4)
- [ ] Padlock
- [ ] Paper bag
- [ ] Periscope
- [ ] Pointed hats (3)
- [ ] Propellers (2)
- [ ] Rabbit
- [ ] Ring of fire
- [ ] Sailor
- [ ] Santa Claus
- [ ] Straw hat
- [ ] Unhappy face
- [ ] Unicorn
- [ ] Whip

Look for **Laura**
at
School
and...

- ☐ Basketball
- ☐ Birdhouse
- ☐ Bookend
- ☐ Boot
- ☐ Clock
- ☐ Cupcake
- ☐ Dog
- ☐ Drum set
- ☐ Earmuffs
- ☐ Eyeglasses (3)
- ☐ Fork
- ☐ Globe
- ☐ Golf club
- ☐ Hair bows (5)
- ☐ Joke book
- ☐ Jump rope
- ☐ Mitten
- ☐ Pen
- ☐ Pencils (4)
- ☐ Rabbit
- ☐ Scarf
- ☐ Soccer ball
- ☐ Sock
- ☐ Straw hat
- ☐ Teddy bear
- ☐ Three-legged stool
- ☐ Tic-tac-toe
- ☐ Top hat
- ☐ TV set

DETECT DONALD   FIND FRANKIE   SEARCH FOR SUSIE   LOOK FOR LAURA

SEARCH FOR SUSIE

Search for Susie in the Big Fun Park and...

- [ ] Baby dinosaurs (2)
- [ ] Bench
- [ ] Billy goat
- [ ] Blue jay
- [ ] Boot
- [ ] Cactus
- [ ] Cat
- [ ] Coffeepot
- [ ] Dollar sign
- [ ] Elephants (3)
- [ ] Fire hydrant
- [ ] Giraffes (2)
- [ ] Hamburgers (3)
- [ ] Kite
- [ ] Mice (2)
- [ ] Monkey
- [ ] Necklace
- [ ] Owl
- [ ] Pelican
- [ ] Penguin
- [ ] Periscopes (2)
- [ ] Pigs (4)
- [ ] Sailboat
- [ ] Sailor hat
- [ ] Scarecrow
- [ ] Stars (6)
- [ ] Wagon
- [ ] Susie's mom
- [ ] Telescope
- [ ] Unicorn
- [ ] Wolf

Search for Susie
at the
Water
Ride
and...

- ☐ Apple
- ☐ Beach ball
- ☐ Bib
- ☐ Bull
- ☐ Candles (2)
- ☐ Cats (2)
- ☐ Earring
- ☐ Elephants (2)
- ☐ Fishing pole
- ☐ Gorilla
- ☐ Hearts (2)
- ☐ Hot dog
- ☐ Kangaroo
- ☐ Paper bag
- ☐ Parrot
- ☐ Pencil
- ☐ Periscope
- ☐ Picnic basket
- ☐ Pitcher
- ☐ Puddles (4)
- ☐ Rabbits (2)
- ☐ Scuba diver
- ☐ Sheep
- ☐ Snakes (2)
- ☐ Sunglasses (2)
- ☐ Tents (3)
- ☐ Tire
- ☐ Turtle
- ☐ Wooden leg

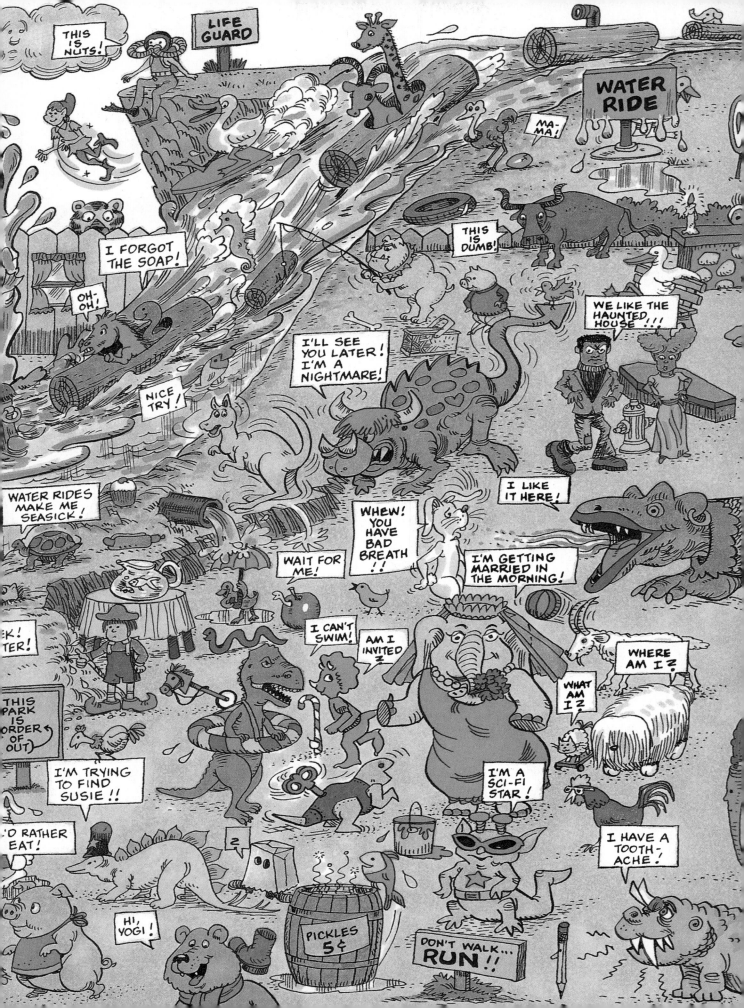

Search for Susie at the Fun House and...

- ☐ Airplane
- ☐ Alligator
- ☐ Anchor
- ☐ Banana peel
- ☐ Baseball cap
- ☐ Bowling ball
- ☐ Cactus
- ☐ Candle
- ☐ Chef's hat
- ☐ Clothespin
- ☐ Comb
- ☐ Curtains
- ☐ Diving board
- ☐ Flowers (2)
- ☐ Football
- ☐ Giraffes (2)
- ☐ Lamp
- ☐ Lollipop
- ☐ Lost boots (2)
- ☐ Masks (2)
- ☐ Mice (2)
- ☐ Pinocchio
- ☐ Pot
- ☐ Rabbits (3)
- ☐ Sailor hat
- ☐ Television
- ☐ Turtles (2)
- ☐ Vase
- ☐ Wall clocks (2)
- ☐ Wristwatch

Search for **Susie** at the **Ferris Wheel** and...

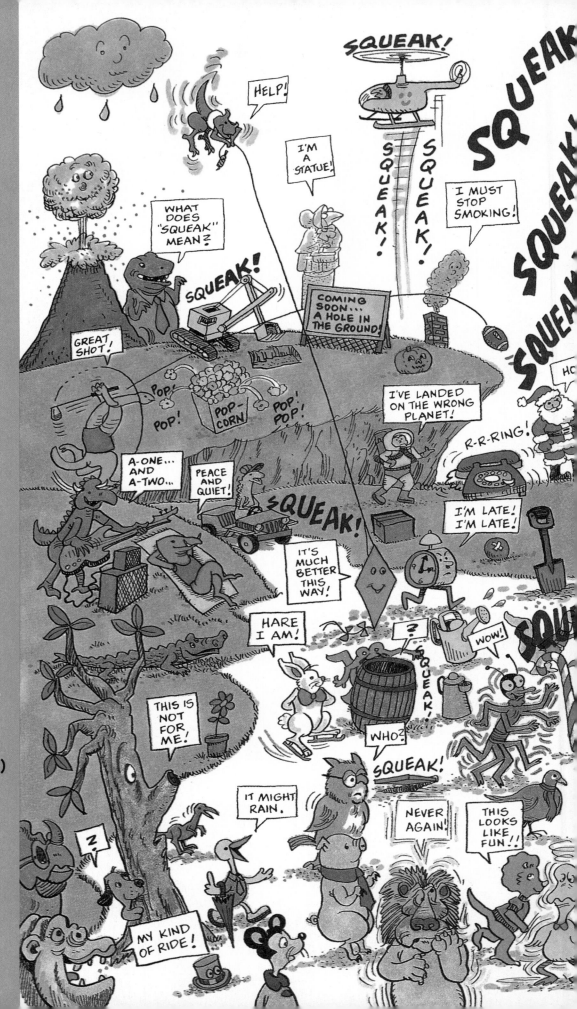

Search for Susie
on the
Rock and
Roller Coaster
and...

- ☐ Barbell
- ☐ Beach ball
- ☐ Bowling ball
- ☐ Buffalo
- ☐ Cactus
- ☐ Candy cane
- ☐ Doghouse
- ☐ Dogs (2)
- ☐ Eight ball
- ☐ Elephants (2)
- ☐ Fisher-cat
- ☐ Football
- ☐ Giraffes (3)
- ☐ Hockey stick
- ☐ Hot dog
- ☐ Ice-cream cone
- ☐ Mailbox
- ☐ Mice (3)
- ☐ Pencil
- ☐ Periscope
- ☐ Pigs (2)
- ☐ Pot
- ☐ Snake
- ☐ Swings
- ☐ Target
- ☐ Telescope
- ☐ Tin can
- ☐ Train engine
- ☐ Turtles (2)
- ☐ Well

Search for Susie on the
Bumper Cars
and...

- [ ] Alligator
- [ ] Automobile
- [ ] Banana peel
- [ ] Baseball cap
- [ ] Birds (3)
- [ ] Bow ties (2)
- [ ] Easel
- [ ] Elephants (2)
- [ ] Football player
- [ ] Lions (2)
- [ ] Manhole
- [ ] Necklace
- [ ] Old shoe
- [ ] Paintbrush
- [ ] "Pay Toll Here"
- [ ] Propeller
- [ ] Rope
- [ ] Sailboat
- [ ] Scarves (2)
- [ ] Seal
- [ ] Snake
- [ ] Sneaker car
- [ ] Straw
- [ ] Surfboard
- [ ] Table
- [ ] Tiger
- [ ] Top hat
- [ ] Tuba
- [ ] Turtle

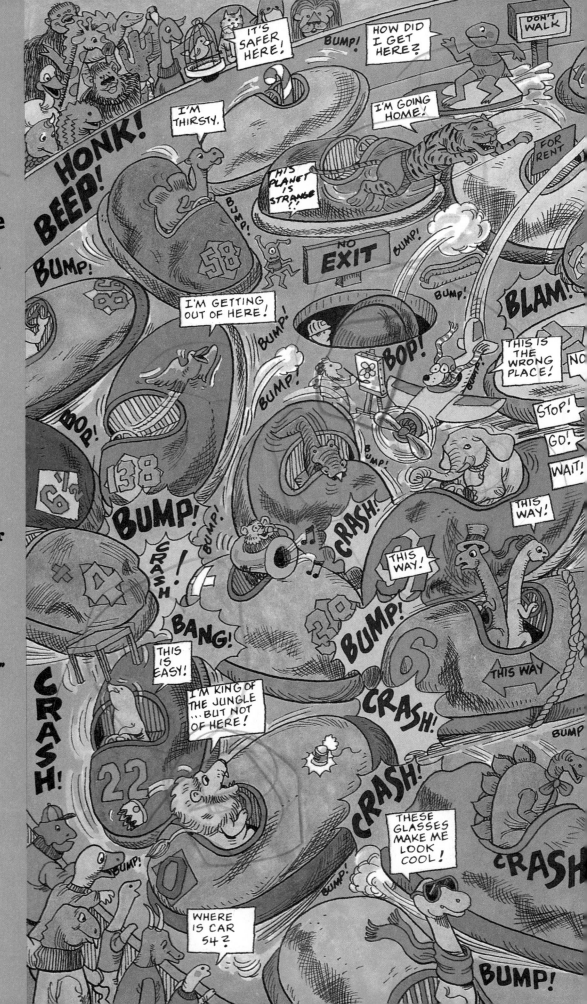

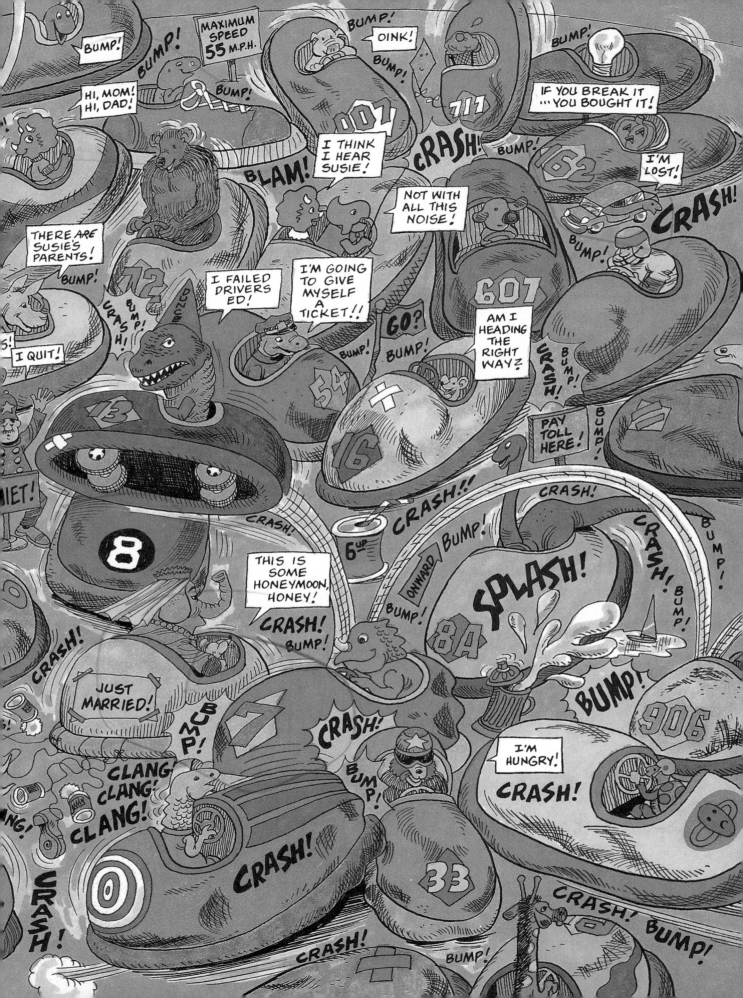

Search for Susie
on the
Giant Swings
and...

- [ ] Arrow
- [ ] Bears (2)
- [ ] Birdcage
- [ ] Bowling ball
- [ ] Candle
- [ ] Cat
- [ ] Dart
- [ ] Dogs (3)
- [ ] Elephants (2)
- [ ] Fishhook
- [ ] Football helmet
- [ ] Hot dog
- [ ] Ice skate
- [ ] Lamps (2)
- [ ] Lollipop
- [ ] Lost sneaker
- [ ] Magic lamp
- [ ] Monkey
- [ ] Mouse
- [ ] Penguin
- [ ] Propeller hat
- [ ] Rocket
- [ ] Scissors
- [ ] Soccer ball
- [ ] Sock
- [ ] Superhero
- [ ] Yo-yo

SEARCH FOR SUSIE　　LOOK FOR LAURA　　DETECT DONALD　　FIND FRANKIE

WHERE ARE THEY?

FIND FREDDIE: AROUND THE WORLD

TIME TRAVELER

LOOK FOR LISA: TIME TRAVELER

WHERE'S WENDY?

SEARCH FOR SYLVESTER

Travel the world to find Freddie.

Travel through time to look for Lisa.

Search high and low for Sylvester.

Find out where Wendy could possibly be!

FREDDIE

LISA

WENDY

SYLVESTER

FIND FREDDIE AROUND THE WORLD

Find **Freddie**
in the
United
States
and...

- [ ] Alien
- [ ] Barbell
- [ ] Baseball player
- [ ] Beavers (2)
- [ ] Binoculars
- [ ] Carrot
- [ ] Cheese
- [ ] Cook
- [ ] Doctor
- [ ] Dog bone
- [ ] Dogs (2)
- [ ] Elephant
- [ ] Fire hydrant
- [ ] Football player
- [ ] Ice-cream cone
- [ ] Mice (3)
- [ ] Movie camera
- [ ] Octopus
- [ ] Palm trees (4)
- [ ] Rabbits (2)
- [ ] Skier
- [ ] Snake
- [ ] Snowman
- [ ] Stop sign
- [ ] Tent
- [ ] Trash can
- [ ] White House

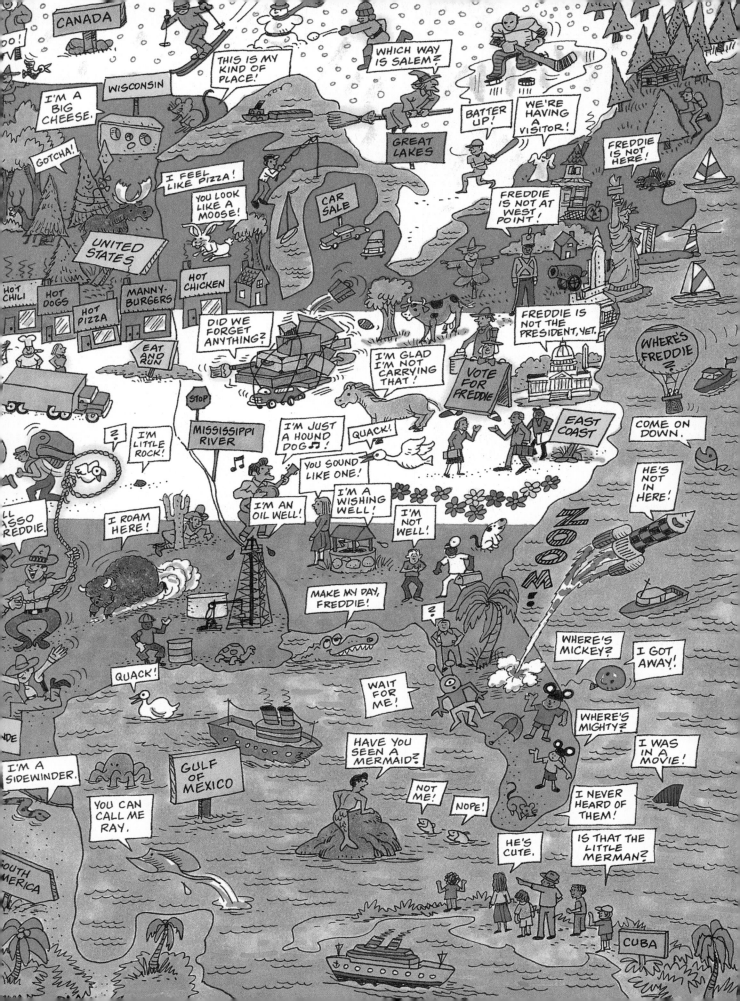

Find Freddie in this **Winter Wonderland** and...

- [ ] Balloon
- [ ] Banana peel
- [ ] Caveman
- [ ] Deer
- [ ] Dogsled
- [ ] Dogs (3)
- [ ] Hockey player
- [ ] Ice skates (5)
- [ ] Leprechaun
- [ ] Maple syrup
- [ ] Moose
- [ ] Periscope
- [ ] Police officer
- [ ] Pumpkin
- [ ] Rabbit
- [ ] Raccoon
- [ ] Refrigerator
- [ ] Sailboat
- [ ] Santa Claus
- [ ] Skiers (2)
- [ ] Spear
- [ ] Superhero
- [ ] Telescope
- [ ] Tent
- [ ] Tin man
- [ ] Tree stumps (4)
- [ ] TV camera
- [ ] Viking
- [ ] Walrus

Find Freddie in the **British Isles** and...

- ☐ Artist
- ☐ Baby carriage
- ☐ Balloon
- ☐ Bicycle
- ☐ Big Ben
- ☐ Bow & arrow
- ☐ Clouds (2)
- ☐ Cow
- ☐ Double-decker bus
- ☐ Ducks (2)
- ☐ Four-leaf clovers (3)
- ☐ Fox
- ☐ Goalpost
- ☐ Golfer
- ☐ Hammock
- ☐ Horse
- ☐ Hot-air balloon
- ☐ Loaf of bread
- ☐ Miners (2)
- ☐ Mouse
- ☐ Mushroom
- ☐ Musical notes (4)
- ☐ Pencil
- ☐ Rainbow
- ☐ Scarecrow
- ☐ Scooter
- ☐ Shovel
- ☐ Socks
- ☐ Surfer
- ☐ Wheelbarrow

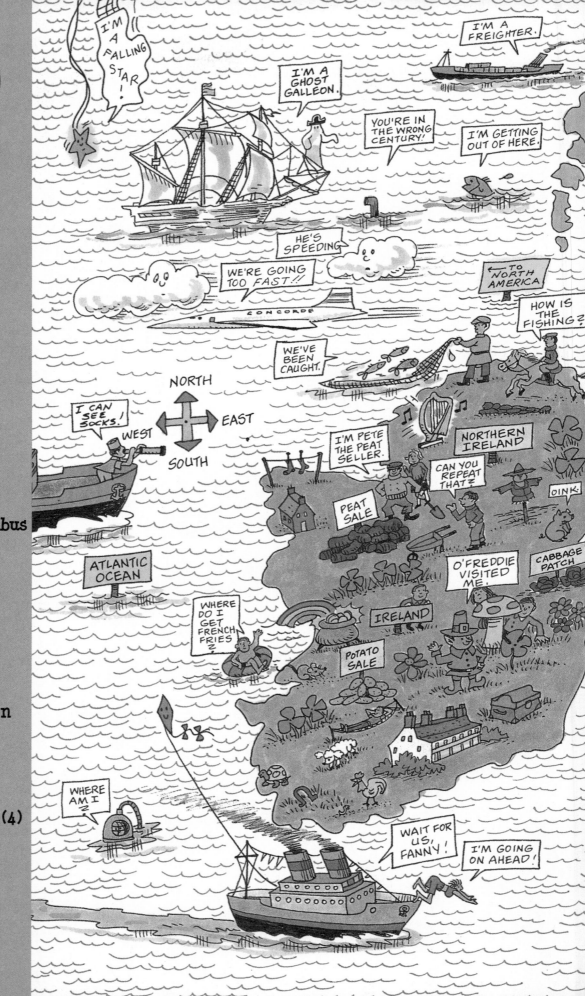

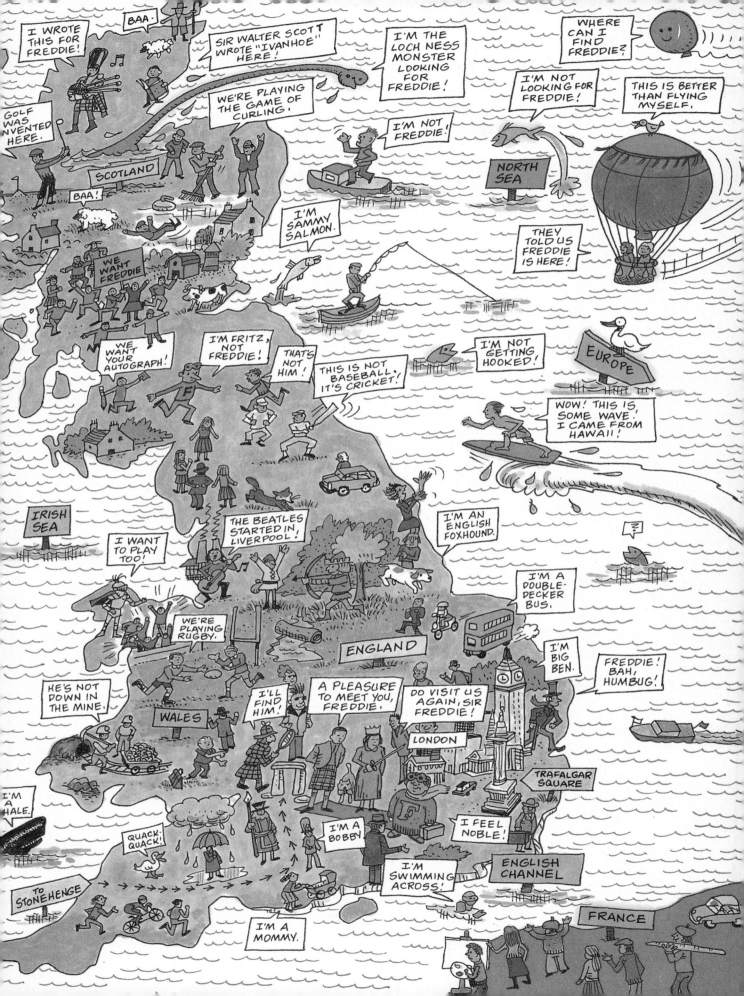

Find Freddie in the Land Down Under and...

- [ ] Apples (7)
- [ ] Barbecue
- [ ] Boot
- [ ] Cloud
- [ ] Cow
- [ ] Crocodile
- [ ] Doctor
- [ ] Eggs (4)
- [ ] Emu
- [ ] Fishing poles (2)
- [ ] Ghost
- [ ] Guitar
- [ ] Lifeguard
- [ ] Message in a bottle
- [ ] Octopus
- [ ] Penguin
- [ ] Platypus
- [ ] Sailboats (2)
- [ ] Shark fins (5)
- [ ] Skiers (2)
- [ ] Snake
- [ ] Snowman
- [ ] Surfboards (9)
- [ ] Tasmanian devil
- [ ] Tennis rackets (4)
- [ ] Tire

Find Freddie in this **African Adventure Land** and...

- ☑ Alligator
- ☐ Ant
- ☐ Banana
- ☐ Bone
- ☐ Cat
- ☐ Crown
- ☐ Diamonds
- ☐ Donkey
- ☐ Egg
- ☐ Fishing nets (2)
- ☐ Fishing pole
- ☐ Flamingo
- ☐ Message in a bottle
- ☐ Moon
- ☐ Mug
- ☐ Mushroom
- ☐ Palm trees (3)
- ☐ Pyramid
- ☐ Rowboats (4)
- ☐ Santa Claus
- ☐ Seal
- ☐ Sunglasses (4)
- ☐ Surfboard
- ☐ Telescope
- ☐ Turtle
- ☐ Zebra

Find Freddie in this **Blistery Blizzard** and...

- ☐ Airplane
- ☐ Aliens (2)
- ☐ Baseball
- ☐ Box
- ☐ Campfire
- ☐ Circus tents (2)
- ☐ Easel
- ☐ Football
- ☐ Heart
- ☐ Helicopter
- ☐ Ice castle
- ☐ Ice skates (6)
- ☐ Jack-o'-lantern
- ☐ Kangaroo
- ☐ Kite
- ☐ Magic carpet
- ☐ Paintbrush
- ☐ Periscope
- ☐ Santa Claus
- ☐ Skis (4)
- ☐ Sleds (5)
- ☐ Spaceship
- ☐ Stars (2)
- ☐ Tennis racket
- ☐ Tin man
- ☐ Tombstone
- ☐ Top hats (2)

Find Freddie in South America and...

- ☐ Angel
- ☐ Ant
- ☐ Banana peel
- ☐ Beach ball
- ☐ Beehive
- ☐ Briefcase
- ☐ Candy bar
- ☐ Chinchilla
- ☐ Coconut
- ☐ Condor
- ☐ Dracula
- ☐ Flamingos (3)
- ☐ Flying bats (2)
- ☐ Iguana
- ☐ Jaguar
- ☐ Manatee
- ☐ Mouse
- ☐ Musical notes (3)
- ☐ Ostrich
- ☐ Penguin
- ☐ Pig
- ☐ Shark fins (2)
- ☐ Skull
- ☐ Spider
- ☐ Tires (2)
- ☐ Top hat
- ☐ Toucans (2)
- ☐ Tuba
- ☐ Waterfall

Find Freddie in
Central America
and...

- ☐ Banana tree
- ☐ Birdbath
- ☐ Bones (2)
- ☐ Broom
- ☐ Bucket
- ☐ Bull
- ☐ Cactus
- ☐ Camera
- ☐ Flying bats (2)
- ☐ Football
- ☐ Golfer
- ☐ Heart
- ☐ Hot-air balloon
- ☐ Kite
- ☐ Medal
- ☐ Periscope
- ☐ Pie
- ☐ Piggy bank
- ☐ Pizza
- ☐ Police officer
- ☐ Princess
- ☐ Rabbits (2)
- ☐ Sailboats (4)
- ☐ Snakes (2)
- ☐ Turtle
- ☐ Water skis
- ☐ Whale
- ☐ Wrench

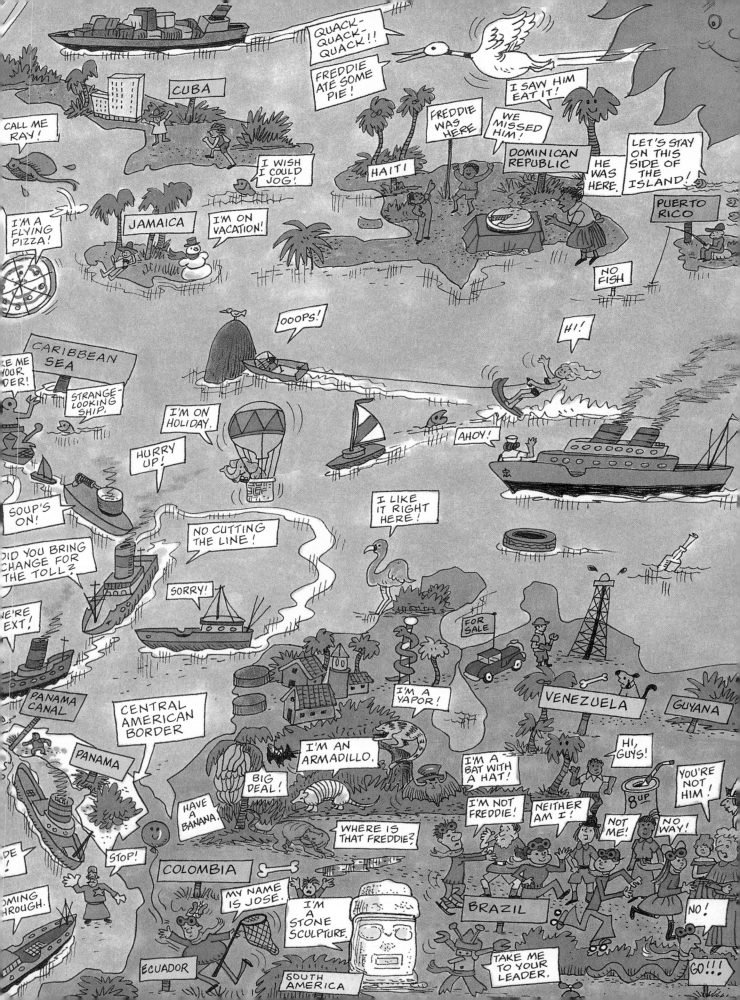

Find Freddie on his Last Stop and...

- ☐ Alarm clock
- ☐ Apple
- ☐ Baseball player
- ☐ Beaver
- ☐ Cactus (2)
- ☐ Carrot
- ☐ Castle
- ☐ Cow
- ☐ Cowboys (2)
- ☐ Dogs (3)
- ☐ Hose
- ☐ Mermaid
- ☐ Moose
- ☐ Octopus
- ☐ Painted egg
- ☐ Paper airplane
- ☐ Parachute
- ☐ Periscope
- ☐ Refrigerator
- ☐ Sailboats (2)
- ☐ Sherlock Holmes
- ☐ Skunk
- ☐ Snowball
- ☐ Suit of armor
- ☐ Tents (2)
- ☐ Trash can
- ☐ Whales (2)
- ☐ Witch

Find Freddie and...

- ☐ Apple
- ☐ Baseball bat
- ☐ Birdcage
- ☐ Bucket
- ☐ Candle
- ☐ Cupcake
- ☐ Fire hydrant
- ☐ Flower
- ☐ Football helmet
- ☐ Frog
- ☐ Gift
- ☐ Hearts (2)
- ☐ Ice-cream cone
- ☐ Jump rope
- ☐ Medal
- ☐ Mitten
- ☐ Moon
- ☐ Mouse
- ☐ Pencil
- ☐ Pizza box
- ☐ Plate
- ☐ Rocking chair
- ☐ Turtle

LOOK FOR LISA: TIME TRAVELER

Look for **Lisa** in
Prehistoric Times
and...

- ☐ Baby carriage
- ☐ Candle
- ☐ Cherry
- ☐ Clothespin
- ☐ Dinosaur egg
- ☐ Faucet
- ☐ Four-leaf clover
- ☐ Hammer
- ☐ Hot chocolate
- ☐ Life preserver
- ☐ Message in a bottle
- ☐ Necklace
- ☐ Necktie
- ☐ "No U Turn"
- ☐ Palm trees (2)
- ☐ Periscope
- ☐ Piggy bank
- ☐ Pizza
- ☐ Ring
- ☐ Scarecrow
- ☐ Skateboard
- ☐ Stars (2)
- ☐ Swimming duck
- ☐ Tire
- ☐ Toothbrush
- ☐ Volcanoes (2)
- ☐ Wooden wheel

Look for **Lisa** at this **Historic Happening** and...

Look for Lisa as she Rocks and Rolls and...

- [ ] Accordion
- [ ] Bandanna
- [ ] Bow tie
- [ ] Broken nose
- [ ] Cameras (5)
- [ ] Cymbals
- [ ] Earmuffs
- [ ] Elephant
- [ ] Feather
- [ ] Fiddle
- [ ] Flags (2)
- [ ] Flying bat
- [ ] Football helmet
- [ ] Harmonica
- [ ] Horse
- [ ] King Kong
- [ ] Ladder
- [ ] Mailbox
- [ ] Microphones (2)
- [ ] Paper airplane
- [ ] Propeller hat
- [ ] Red wagon
- [ ] Scarf
- [ ] Speaker
- [ ] Stage lights (6)
- [ ] Submarine
- [ ] Trumpet
- [ ] Turtle

Look for **Lisa** in these
Cavernous
Craters
and...

- ☐ Axe
- ☐ Banana
- ☐ Bucket
- ☐ Car
- ☐ Clown
- ☐ Coffeepot
- ☐ Cup
- ☐ Duck
- ☐ Earth
- ☐ Envelope
- ☐ Fish
- ☐ Flashlight
- ☐ Heart
- ☐ Key
- ☐ Kite
- ☐ Ladder
- ☐ Mouse
- ☐ Penguin
- ☐ Pig
- ☐ Pumpkin
- ☐ Ring
- ☐ Saw
- ☐ Shovel
- ☐ Stamp
- ☐ Stars (4)
- ☐ Stool
- ☐ Toothbrush
- ☐ Turtle

Look for **Lisa** in the **Ocean** and...

- ☐ Baby
- ☐ Barrel
- ☐ Baseball bat
- ☐ Basketball
- ☐ Boot
- ☐ Bucket
- ☐ Captain's hat
- ☐ Elephant
- ☐ Fish (3)
- ☐ Guitar
- ☐ Harp
- ☐ Heart
- ☐ Homework
- ☐ Hot-air balloon
- ☐ Ice-cream cone
- ☐ Key
- ☐ Oars (5)
- ☐ Painting
- ☐ Palm tree
- ☐ Scuba diver
- ☐ Shark fins (2)
- ☐ Slice of watermelon
- ☐ Sock
- ☐ Surfer
- ☐ Television
- ☐ Tin can
- ☐ Tire
- ☐ Tree

Look for Lisa at Thomas Edison's Lab and...

Look for Lisa among these Friendly Aliens and...

- ☐ Airplane
- ☐ Basketball hoop
- ☐ Bowling ball
- ☐ Briefcase
- ☐ Cactus
- ☐ Crayon
- ☐ Cup
- ☐ Desk lamp
- ☐ Donut
- ☐ Envelope
- ☐ Flower
- ☐ Hamburger
- ☐ Hose
- ☐ Hot dog
- ☐ Musical note
- ☐ "No Parking"
- ☐ Paintbrush
- ☐ Pencils (2)
- ☐ Pirates (2)
- ☐ Pyramid
- ☐ Straw
- ☐ Target
- ☐ Television
- ☐ Top hat
- ☐ Train
- ☐ Trash can
- ☐ Trees (3)
- ☐ Yo-yo

Look for Lisa at the Magic Show and...

- ☐ Apple
- ☐ Barbell
- ☐ Barrel
- ☐ Beard
- ☐ Box
- ☐ Burned-out light bulbs (2)
- ☐ Dragon
- ☐ Elephants (2)
- ☐ Football
- ☐ Graduation cap
- ☐ Headband
- ☐ Heart
- ☐ Jack-o'-lantern
- ☐ Key
- ☐ Knight
- ☐ Leaf
- ☐ Mouse
- ☐ Palm tree
- ☐ Puppy
- ☐ Purple hat
- ☐ Rabbit
- ☐ Sandbag
- ☐ Snake
- ☐ Top hat
- ☐ Trapdoors (2)
- ☐ Weight lifter
- ☐ Whale

Look for Lisa and...

- [ ] Baseball bat
- [ ] Bird
- [ ] Bottle
- [ ] Broom
- [ ] Cactus
- [ ] Can
- [ ] Cane
- [ ] Fire hydrant
- [ ] Fish
- [ ] Flowers (2)
- [ ] Hammers (2)
- [ ] Kite
- [ ] Moon
- [ ] Octopus
- [ ] Rabbit
- [ ] Saw
- [ ] Scarves (2)
- [ ] Snake
- [ ] Sun
- [ ] Tire
- [ ] Top hat
- [ ] Turtle
- [ ] Wreath

Search for Sylvester at this
Mad Mall
and...

- ☐ Astronaut
- ☐ Balloon
- ☐ Barber pole
- ☐ Bone
- ☐ Bride
- ☐ Briefcase
- ☐ Cat
- ☐ Cowboy hat
- ☐ Feathers (2)
- ☐ Fish (2)
- ☐ King
- ☐ Ladder
- ☐ Manhole
- ☐ Moon
- ☐ Mouse
- ☐ Musical note
- ☐ Parachute
- ☐ Pizza
- ☐ Robin Hood
- ☐ Sailboat
- ☐ Scarecrow
- ☐ Shopping bag
- ☐ Skier
- ☐ Stool
- ☐ Stuffed elephant
- ☐ Tin man
- ☐ Top hat
- ☐ Winter hats (2)

Search for Sylvester in this
Fun-Filled Playground
and...

- ☐ Arrows (3)
- ☐ Ballerina
- ☐ Banana peel
- ☐ Beach ball
- ☐ Birdcage
- ☐ Birdhouse
- ☐ Birds (4)
- ☐ Bowling pin
- ☐ Cactus
- ☐ Cannon
- ☐ Diploma
- ☐ Dracula
- ☐ Ducklings (4)
- ☐ Eight ball
- ☐ Fire hydrant
- ☐ Flying bat
- ☐ Hockey stick
- ☐ Lamp
- ☐ Newspapers (2)
- ☐ Paint bucket
- ☐ Police officer
- ☐ Propeller hat
- ☐ Rooster
- ☐ Saws (2)
- ☐ Shovel
- ☐ Superhero
- ☐ Turtle

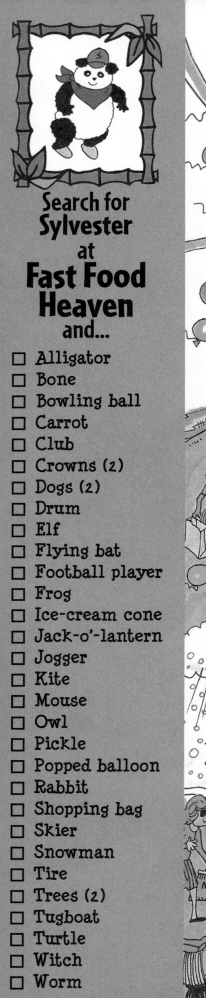

Search for **Sylvester** at the **Zany Zoo** and...

- ☐ Baseball bat
- ☐ Baseball caps (4)
- ☐ Bow tie
- ☐ Camel
- ☐ Fish
- ☐ Football
- ☐ Girl with pigtails
- ☐ Kangaroo
- ☐ Little Red Riding Hood
- ☐ Neckties (3)
- ☐ Owl
- ☐ Parrot
- ☐ Pig
- ☐ Pine tree
- ☐ Rabbit
- ☐ Raccoon
- ☐ Scarf
- ☐ School bus
- ☐ Sea horse
- ☐ Seal
- ☐ Shovel
- ☐ Spoon
- ☐ Telescope
- ☐ Top hat
- ☐ Toy turtle
- ☐ Trash can
- ☐ Turtle
- ☐ Waiter

Search for **Sylvester** in this **Alphabetical School** and...

Search for Sylvester at this Spooky Mansion and...

- ☐ Arrows (2)
- ☐ Book
- ☐ Brush
- ☐ Bucket
- ☐ Candle
- ☐ Carrot
- ☐ Cauldron
- ☐ Curtains
- ☐ Flower
- ☐ Flying bat
- ☐ Football
- ☐ Ghost
- ☐ Hammer
- ☐ Lawn mower
- ☐ Letter
- ☐ Old tire
- ☐ Piano keys
- ☐ Shovel
- ☐ Skulls (2)
- ☐ Spiderweb
- ☐ Sword
- ☐ Tin can
- ☐ Trash can lid
- ☐ Vulture
- ☐ Wagon
- ☐ Watering can
- ☐ Witch

Search for Sylvester at Detective Donald's Digs and...

- ☐ Broken pencils (3)
- ☐ Calendar
- ☐ Can
- ☐ Candles (3)
- ☐ Chalk
- ☐ Chalkboard
- ☐ Cheese
- ☐ Comb
- ☐ Diploma
- ☐ Fan
- ☐ Fishing pole
- ☐ Jacket
- ☐ Key
- ☐ Ladder
- ☐ Lamp
- ☐ Medal
- ☐ Nail
- ☐ Paint bucket
- ☐ Roller skate
- ☐ Screwdriver
- ☐ Shovel
- ☐ Skull
- ☐ Snake
- ☐ Stack of envelopes
- ☐ Sword
- ☐ Tack
- ☐ Top hat
- ☐ Trunk

Search for
Sylvester
at this
Silly Circus
and...

- ☐ Balloon with star
- ☐ Barrel
- ☐ Cactus
- ☐ Cake
- ☐ Camel
- ☐ Cannon
- ☐ Clothespins (3)
- ☐ Clowns (4)
- ☐ Crayon
- ☐ Firefighter
- ☐ Flowerpot
- ☐ Light bulb
- ☐ Mice (2)
- ☐ Necktie
- ☐ Party hat
- ☐ Pinocchio
- ☐ Pizza
- ☐ Police officer
- ☐ Skateboard
- ☐ Snowman
- ☐ Spoon
- ☐ Stars (5)
- ☐ Teacup
- ☐ Tin man
- ☐ Unicycle
- ☐ Witch
- ☐ Wizard hat
- ☐ Worm

Search for Sylvester as he Soars Through the Sky and...

- ☐ Ape
- ☐ Banana
- ☐ Baseball bat
- ☐ Bathtub
- ☐ Bird
- ☐ Bow
- ☐ Carrot
- ☐ Cupcake
- ☐ Fishermen (2)
- ☐ Flowers (4)
- ☐ Flying bat
- ☐ Football player
- ☐ Guitar
- ☐ Moon
- ☐ Pot
- ☐ Scarecrow
- ☐ Scarf
- ☐ Shovel
- ☐ Spaceship
- ☐ Stars (3)
- ☐ Sunglasses
- ☐ Target
- ☐ Teapot
- ☐ Tent
- ☐ TV antenna
- ☐ Watering can
- ☐ Witch

Search for Sylvester in

Bamboo Town

and...

- ☐ Balloons (2)
- ☐ Brooms (2)
- ☐ Drum
- ☐ Eyeglasses (2)
- ☐ Fire hydrants (2)
- ☐ Football
- ☐ Football player
- ☐ Ghost
- ☐ Gift
- ☐ Hard hats (2)
- ☐ Heart
- ☐ Horseshoe
- ☐ Ice-cream cones (2)
- ☐ Jump rope
- ☐ Kangaroo
- ☐ Knight
- ☐ Mask
- ☐ Medal
- ☐ Octopus
- ☐ Pencil
- ☐ Periscope
- ☐ Record
- ☐ Socks (3)
- ☐ Stool
- ☐ Straw
- ☐ Telescope
- ☐ Wizard
- ☐ Worm

Search for Sylvester and...

- ☐ Apple
- ☐ Bamboo shoot
- ☐ Baseball
- ☐ Bone
- ☐ Candle
- ☐ Cane
- ☐ Carrot
- ☐ Cupcake
- ☐ Drum
- ☐ Fire hydrant
- ☐ Flag
- ☐ Flowers (10)
- ☐ Football
- ☐ Horn
- ☐ Kite
- ☐ Leaf
- ☐ Lock
- ☐ Moon
- ☐ Paintbrush
- ☐ Screwdriver
- ☐ Spoon
- ☐ Top hat
- ☐ Turtle

Find Wendy at
Witchville
High School
and...

- [ ] Apple
- [ ] Axe
- [ ] Baseball bat
- [ ] Bear
- [ ] Bell
- [ ] Blimp
- [ ] Bowling ball
- [ ] Cauldrons (2)
- [ ] Dog
- [ ] Flying bats (2)
- [ ] Football
- [ ] Green hand
- [ ] Headless man
- [ ] Mask
- [ ] Mushrooms (3)
- [ ] One-eyed monsters (2)
- [ ] Pencil
- [ ] Piece of paper
- [ ] Scarecrow
- [ ] Shovel
- [ ] Skateboard
- [ ] Tire
- [ ] Tombstones (3)
- [ ] Turtle
- [ ] TV antenna
- [ ] Unicorn
- [ ] Walking tree
- [ ] Worm

Find Wendy in the
Lunchroom
and...

- [ ] Apple
- [ ] Bird
- [ ] Broken nose
- [ ] Cactus
- [ ] Candle
- [ ] Cat
- [ ] Chick
- [ ] Cookbook
- [ ] Crystal ball
- [ ] Cymbals (2)
- [ ] Drum
- [ ] Flower
- [ ] Football
- [ ] Frying pans (3)
- [ ] Graduate
- [ ] Lighthouse
- [ ] Musical notes (3)
- [ ] Paper airplane
- [ ] Plate of cookies
- [ ] Santa Claus
- [ ] Skull
- [ ] Snakes (2)
- [ ] Straw
- [ ] Teapot
- [ ] Trash can
- [ ] Turtle
- [ ] Volcano
- [ ] Yellow hand
- [ ] Yellow sock

Look for Wendy during Final Exams and...

- ☐ Ball of yarn
- ☐ Balloon
- ☐ Baseball cap
- ☐ Broken mirror
- ☐ Broken pot
- ☐ Brooms (2)
- ☐ Cheese
- ☐ Chicken
- ☐ Clipboards (4)
- ☐ Cloud
- ☐ Coonskin cap
- ☐ Doctor
- ☐ Duck
- ☐ Elephant
- ☐ Flying bats (3)
- ☐ Football
- ☐ Heart
- ☐ Jack-o'-lantern
- ☐ Lost mitten
- ☐ Magic lamp
- ☐ Mouse
- ☐ Pencil
- ☐ Pogo stick
- ☐ Saw
- ☐ Skulls (2)
- ☐ Stool
- ☐ Tombstone
- ☐ Trunk
- ☐ Worm

Hunt for Wendy at Graduation and...

- [ ] Barbell
- [ ] Bones (2)
- [ ] Broken mirror
- [ ] Brooms (3)
- [ ] Can
- [ ] Candle
- [ ] Cracked egg
- [ ] Dog
- [ ] Drum
- [ ] Flying bats (2)
- [ ] Ghost
- [ ] Graduation cap
- [ ] Guitar
- [ ] Kite
- [ ] Marshmallow
- [ ] Moons (2)
- [ ] Panda
- [ ] Pumpkins (2)
- [ ] Robot
- [ ] Sled
- [ ] Target
- [ ] Tire
- [ ] Tombstones (13)
- [ ] Toolbox
- [ ] Tuba
- [ ] Turtle
- [ ] Umbrella
- [ ] Wizard
- [ ] Worm

Find Wendy in
Count Dracula's Living Room
and...

- ☒ Airplane
- ☐ Baseball bat
- ☐ Birdcage
- ☐ Book
- ☐ Brooms (3)
- ☐ Chair
- ☐ Chicken
- ☐ Cracked egg
- ☐ Crayon
- ☐ Dustpan
- ☐ Globe
- ☐ Mice (3)
- ☐ Mousehole
- ☐ Mummy
- ☐ Owl
- ☐ Paintbrush
- ☐ Piano keys
- ☐ Pig
- ☐ Pitcher
- ☐ Spiderweb
- ☐ Teacup
- ☐ Teapot
- ☐ Telephone
- ☐ Top hat
- ☐ Umbrellas (3)
- ☐ Vacuum
- ☐ Worm
- ☐ Wreath

Search for **Wendy**
in
Dr. Frankenstein's
Laboratory
and...

- ☐ Ball of yarn
- ☐ Banana
- ☐ Baseball cap
- ☐ Bird
- ☐ Boot
- ☐ Bow
- ☐ Bucket
- ☐ Candles (2)
- ☐ Cheese
- ☐ Clock
- ☐ Eight ball
- ☐ Eyeglasses
- ☐ Flowers (2)
- ☐ Flying bat
- ☐ Fork
- ☐ Hammer
- ☐ Heart
- ☐ Lips
- ☐ Mask
- ☐ Mice (4)
- ☐ Needle & thread
- ☐ Pig
- ☐ Pizza
- ☐ Present
- ☐ Pumpkin
- ☐ Saw
- ☐ Spoon
- ☐ Stars (4)
- ☐ Stool
- ☐ Watermelon

Hunt for Wendy in the Mummy's Tomb and...

- [ ] "1st Prize" ribbon
- [ ] Bell
- [ ] Butterfly
- [ ] Cactus
- [ ] Cherry
- [ ] Cracked pot
- [ ] Duck
- [ ] Fire hydrant
- [ ] Fish
- [ ] Giraffe
- [ ] Key
- [ ] Lion
- [ ] Lobster
- [ ] Moon
- [ ] Mouse
- [ ] Painted egg
- [ ] Ring
- [ ] Rooster
- [ ] Sea horse
- [ ] Seal
- [ ] Spiderweb
- [ ] Tepee
- [ ] Tiger
- [ ] Top hat
- [ ] Trunk
- [ ] Yellow bird
- [ ] Watering can
- [ ] Winter hat